The Friend's Quest

Harshitha Hebbar

Darpan

An Imprint of Prism Books Pvt. Ltd

The Friend's Quest

Harshitha Hebbar

Published by

Darpan - An Imprint of Prism Books Pvt. Ltd.

1865, 32nd Cross, 10th Main,

BSK II Stage, Bengaluru -560 070

Phone: 080-26714108, Telefax : 080-26713979

e-mail : info@prismbooks.com,

Website: www.prismbooks.com

Also at:

Chennai : 044-24311244 prismchennai@prismbooks.com

Hyderabad: 040-27612928 prismhyderabad@prismbooks.com

Kochi : 0484-4000945 prismkochi@prismbooks.com

Kolkata : 033-24297957 prismkolkata@prismbooks.com

Cover design : Sripad Acharya, Bengaluru

ISBN: 978-81-7286-940-3

Price: ₹ 125

Total Pages : 120

Printed at: Sarada Printers, Hyderabad

Foreword

"Imagination beyond Imagination!" that is this debut - novel's author - the little girl! Harshitha!

The narration darts off with a normal vigourous note of a usual middle-school atmosphere : proceeds in a normal pace for some time; and then glides into a venturesome involvement of the friends; then they get to witness the esoteric character, their apporpriate nomenclatures (through out, with the personification by the author) and their suitable behaviourism; drifts the reader along with the characters to the imaginary planer and lands the reader into the realm of clans - to partake and experience the thrill of their exciting explorations. The little girl novelist's inventure imaginations, and their meticulous presentation - denotes - a bright progressive literary domain of acturalization - in her future.

This is demarked as the 1st volume and any reader would eagerly and expectently look forward for the release of Volume 2 and 3 !! and more !

God's blessings are already favoured on her through her future !

Vasundhara Srinivasan

11-4--2015

Preface

The idea for this book lies solely in my imagination. I had a way with words since a young age. Thanks to my overly imaginative mind, when I was trying to invent a new game to play by myself one day. I got an idea which I decided to develop into this story. While writing this story, my brain thought up new ideas. I couldn't fit them all in this story, so I thought of making this book as a trilogy - a series of three books. Be sure to read my next books !

Firstly, I would sincerely like to thank the Prism Books Pvt Ltd., for publishing my first book and the editor Mrs. Anupama for providing me with suggestions and better ways to frame my story.

I would like to express my gratitude towards Mrs Vasundhara Srinivasan for encouraging me.

I want to thank my drawing teacher Mr Suresh from Kenfortes Art Class for supporting me.

The last but most important thanks goes to my family for all the support they lent to me.

I thank you, the readers too, for reading my book. I hope you will enjoy it!

Harshitha Hebbar

Dedicated to my family and to all those who would love to become Ronens!

1

"Arnold? Tell me, what is 9 times 32?"

The Grade 7 students in a school in Heltswood, Vermont, USA, were facing the most boring subject of the year, which also came with the strictest teacher in town - Math. The teacher was thin and bony, with sharp, crescent sort of glasses perched on the end of her nose, and her name was Mrs Fitch.

"235" said Arnold, sleepily. "Uh oh. Arnold, you are going to get into serious trouble. I'm not sure what the correct answer is, but I'm pretty sure that his answer is wrong," whispered a tall boy with brown hair. "He's always sleeping, even when he's awake!" His cousin, Carra, who sat next to him said, amused. "Yeah" answered Ron, who happened to be the tall boy. Josh turned back. Josh and Ronald were best friends. Carra's best friend May sat next to Josh. "What are you chattering about? Don't disturb me. This problem's cracking my head!" Josh frowned at them.

"Arnold! How can 9 times 32 be 235? Its 288! Detention for you!" Mrs. Fitch yelled. "Yikes!" May muttered.

"Detention for you!" Ron mimicked in a silly, high pitched voice.

"Angelie, what is eight times fifteen?" The teacher asked, always sweet towards the boastful girl, giving simple sums to her all the time.

The know-it-all girl stood up with her 'I know everything; you don't' look.

"It's 120, Mrs. Fitch," She said promptly in her irritating, high-pitched voice, holding her head high.

"Blah blah," Ron muttered under his breath.

"Ron-"

The teacher stopped as the bell rang. "Saved by the bell!" Ron said happily as he picked up his books and raced away to the lockers with his friends. May rolled her eyes as she opened her locker and took out her Chemistry books.

They walked over to the Chemistry lab and filed in. The Chemistry teacher, Mr. Louis told them that he was doing a new experiment and a horrible smell filled the room. Ron took the red cap he wore backwards on his head and covered his nose and mouth with it. May backed out of the room. She stood near the door and so, was the first one to see the principal, Mr. Barkins, striding towards them with a thin girl. She had long, chocolate-brown hair and light green eyes, which was unusual. May alerted Josh, who poked Ron and Carra. They came out in time to see the principal telling May to call the rest of the class outside. When the students gathered around him,

"Kids, this is Helen, Helen Baxter. She will be joining your class" he announced. He chose May to show Helen around since she was the gentlest girl in the class. She introduced herself and her friends to Helen. But before she could introduce Ron to her, he strode up with his long legs.

"Hi Helen. I'm Ron, short for Ronald, as you mostly will know. Where do you live? Did you change your school or did you move anywhere here?" Ron blabbered. "Ron" May warned. "What?" he asked. She glared fiercely at him with her deep ocean blue eyes. "Oh, fine," Ron mumbled and he walked away. May smiled sweetly at Helen. "Sorry about that," She said. "He's always like that. One good glare or punch and he'll shut his mouth," Helen laughed. May showed her around, introducing everyone to her.

At the cafeteria, Ron asked Helen another time, "Where are you from? You moved here, didn't you? Do you have any sisters elder than you? Are they as annoying as mine? What's your dad's name? What do you think about Heltswood? Heltswood is the name of this place if you don't know. Did you?" He babbled again, and was going to ask more questions if Josh hadn't clamped his hand over his friend's mouth. "Hmm mmm!" he still tried to get out his questions, but obviously, every one ignored him.

"Yeah, I moved here last week... I'm not really sure of the name of the lane I live in. It's a little far from here. It's like, 15 minutes away," Helen said softly. She didn't answer any of his other questions. Ron raised his eyebrows and tried to walk away, and Josh finally let go, sure that he wouldn't bother them now, and then followed the boy.

Helen followed them, and sat down next to May and Ron. Carra was opposite to them, talking to Merlyn and Meredith, the twins from the other section. Josh was sitting next to Ron, and just eating.

"You are a vegetarian, aren't you?" May asked Helen. She nodded. She was eating a broccoli. "Ditto," May said.

"So," Ron said, swallowing, "what made your family move here?"

"Well, we were in a rent house before, and the owner used to increase the price a lot every month. Soon we realized that if it went on at this rate, we wouldn't be able to pay the rent at all. So we decided to shift," she ate a carrot before continuing, "And we found a suitable house here. And we moved in as soon as possible,"

"Where did you live before?" A boy sitting opposite of them asked.

This question took Helen aback. "I lived in Rook Street, in Crowfield," She said.

"How is it there?" Carra asked.

"Well, it was a nice place, full of trees, and lots of nice people, especially the fat lady who lived next door. She used to burden us with food all the time," Helen laughed.

"Which school did you go to?" Josh asked.

"Umm, I went to a school with a really weird name- Crowfield King Charles school. It is named after Crowfield's first leader, you know, the guy who made Crowfield a good city," Helen explained.

"Who were your best friends there?" The boy sitting in front of them asked.

"Uh, there were three girls, Christina, Kaira and Jasmine. They were my best friends. They were really funny, and nice. Christina and Kaira are actually cousins," Helen said.

***

The next day, though, May did not come to school. Carra decided to meet her after school, but couldn't, so she went the next day, and found May strapped up in bed in her pyjamas.

"May? How are you feeling?" Carra asked worriedly. "A bit better now," May said, petting the white bunny on her stomach.

May had fallen ill, and was ordered by the doctor to stay in bed for a whole week. It was just the second day today, and May was already bed-sick. She was an active girl, and couldn't stay in one place for too long. One hour, and she had to move around. May had caught a fever, which had raised a lot, to 101 degrees.

She stroked Snowflake and smiled when the bunny curled up on her stomach. Carra sat down on the bed, next to May. She stayed there for some time, chatting with May, and then looked at her watch.

"Yikes! I totally forgot!" Carra exclaimed. "My mom told me to go to the market to get veggies for dinner. She'll be waiting. Got to go, May. Sorry. Bye!" She got up and jogged to the door. "Bye, Carra" May said softly. She waved her hand and Carra almost ran out the door.

Carra bumped into Ron in the market, while hurrying to buy potatoes. "Hey, cousin" she said, trying to annoy him. She knew that Ron didn't like the fact that they were cousins. Ron growled at her. At least, it seemed so. But it was actually Pal who growled. Pal was Ron's golden retriever. The dog was growling at an alley cat. But then, he noticed Carra and immediately wagged his furry tail.

"Heya, Pal" she said, petting him. He licked her hand. Then she turned to Ron. "Mom told me to invite you and your family, *including* your sister to dinner tomorrow,"

"Oh man! Why does Jessica have to come?"

"She's your sister, Ron. She's family. Well, bye! Got to go. Mom's waiting," She paid the shopkeeper and skipped down the road, with her bag of vegetables all the way towards her house.

The next morning, they gathered in front of their school.

"Can May come to the pet show next week?" Josh asked Carra. "Yep, she can. She's quite better now. I visited her yesterday,"

"Are you participating?" asked Ron, who had arrived now. "Yeah" Josh and Carra said at the same time. "Good,"

Just then, Helen came jogging to them.

"Hi! Today is my birthday. I'm thirteen now! Here, have a cupcake and this chocolate. My dad said that we will probably have a party sometime," She said happily.

"Cool!"

"Happy birthday, Helen"

"Thanks!"

"Where does May live? I want to give these to her too," Helen asked.

"I'll take you there after school," Carra said.

Just then, Billy, a boy who always argued with everyone came along with his equally snobbish friends.

"Hey guys," he said loudly for Ron and Josh to hear, "You know Ronald and Josh are really sick! They like to hang out with girls!" with that, he ran off, snickering. Ron started to go after them, but Josh stopped him.

"Leave them. It'll do you no good,"

"Oh yes it will! It will certainly give me the pleasure!" Ron snarled angrily and stormed off in the opposite direction of Billy.

"Hey! See you tonight!" Carra called.

The bell rang and they moved on to their classes. They didn't see Ron after recess, but Carra assured them saying, "It's OK. He's going out at lunch. Pal suddenly fell ill, it seems, though I met him yesterday and he was perfectly all right. Needs to take care of the dog, I guess. Jessica's going to some party which she can't miss. Looks like his sister can't come tonight for dinner."

"He did miss an awfully great maths class," Josh said. "He would have been damn happy to see Angelie get scolded by Mrs. Fitch for not paying attention. She must have given up on being teacher's pet!" he said grinning.

"Well, one cannot always be the best, can she?" Helen asked slyly.

"No, I suppose not, Helen. Anyways, do you mind helping me with math homework? Just tell me the answers, will you? At least it will be more helpful for me later!" Carra said.

"Sure, no problem!" Helen said, and the three worked on their math sums together, until Josh's mother came to pick up her son and Carra, and Helen went to her own home.

2

Ron had not been able to come the whole week, since Pal had fallen seriously ill, because of a tick disease. Josh and Carra saw him the next week with May. Carra was so excited to see May that she ran across to hug her accidently knocking Ron over. Carra almost squeezed her friend but drew back when May poked her.

"I know you're happy to see me, Carra. But I don't think you have to squeeze me to death for that," She said, and acted like she was choked and dying.

"OK, OK. I'm sorry," Carra apologised, giggling.

"Have you prepared Snowflake not to get nervous at the show? After all, dogs not like Pal love to chase bunnies," Josh looked at Carra now "and cats,"

"Yeah, yeah. They're prepared," May said, not sounding interested. "What is Pal going to do, Ron? Is he all right, now?" she looked down at Ron, who had not yet stood up. He moaned a bit, massaging his back, and then stood up.

"He's totally fine now. But I'm not really sure what's going to happen at the show. He always gets distracted. But I've taught him to beg, jump, salute, shake, hi five and a few more," Ron said, standing up and dusting his pants. He glared at Carra for making him fall, but she didn't bother.

"Well, well, well! Look who's crying here!" May said looking at the playgrounds of the school.

It was Angelie. Her snooty friends were trying to console her. The four crept closer to hear what the teacher's pet was wailing.

"Mrs. Fitch doesn't even ask me questions any more. No teacher does! They're always paying attention to that new girl, Helen or whatever her stupid name is!" she was sobbing.

The four friends, hidden behind a bush nearby found it very hard not to burst out laughing. They couldn't help a few giggles, though.

"We'll help you, Angel. We'll show that irritating girl and her friends, those meddling foursome, Josh, May, Carra and that extremely annoying Ronald not to mess with us again!" one of her friends said.

"Yikes!" Ron whimpered.

"Hah! Let us see if she can even get close to us!" a new voice suddenly said. They turned around and found Helen crouching behind them.

"God! You scared us!" Josh said.

"C'mon. Let's get out of here," Carra said, trying to wriggle out of the bush.

"Here, let me help you. Your shirt's snagged onto a branch,"

May said and helped Carra out. They filled in May and Ron with what had happened in maths class when the devilish Angel got scolded.

After school, May invited them all to her house. "Mum told me to. It's just because I became all right,"

"Cool!" Ron exclaimed.

"I'll come," Carra said smiling at May but glaring at Ron.

"I can," Josh said.

"I don't think I'm free. I'm afraid I'll have to go to a tiny boy's birthday party. Sorry May," Helen said and went away to where a man was waiting.

"Its fine, Helen. Be at my place at around 5 o'clock. Sleepover, OK?" May said. "My mom's here. See you soon!" she called as she flung her backpack over her shoulder and jogged away.

"Bye!" Carra shouted.

"Thank God she called us over," Ron said leaving out a relieved sigh.

"Why?" asked Josh.

"I can stay away from the Jessica monster!" He said.

"She's not a monster, Ron," Carra said. "She's your sister. Well, bus is leaving. See you!" she ran off to catch her bus.

"Hey, you said you're coming over to my house, right?" Ron asked Josh, staring at a tree where a hawk sat.

"Yep. My dad's too busy to pick me up. So is my mom. What are you staring at?"

"That hawk, I've seen it before. Right there on that tree. It always flies away just after Helen goes,"

"She always leaves at the same time. It can't be just because she left. Maybe it leaves at the same time every day. See? Helen's already left. But it hasn't left," Just then, the hawk spread its wings and flew away. "Or, maybe it did. But still how can you be so sure?" Josh asked.

"It flies away in the same direction as she goes," Ron pointed out.

"Nah. Maybe its tree is that way, or something. Whatever. Why is it so important to you suddenly?"

"Just a question, dear friend. Just a question," Ron said, shaking his head.

3

That evening, they met in May's house.

"Any cookies, mate?" Josh's parrot, Pete asked May.

"Yes, there is, Captain," May laughed, handing over a biscuit to Pete. He gobbled it up.

"Woof! Woof!" Pal barked and ran all around May's legs for a biscuit.

"You want one, too?" she asked and gave one to the dog. As soon as he finished it, he started barking for another cookie. But one hiss from Tabitha, Carra's white Persian cat, silenced Pal. He went and sat in a corner. Pete, finding an opportunity not to be missed, sat on Pal's head.

"If we glare at Ron, he shuts up. If Tabitha hisses at Pal, he shuts up!" Carra joked to May.

"Very funny," Ron snorted. Pal nodded his head vigorously to show his agreement, making Pete fall before he got control and flew away to May. He landed on her outstretched hand.

"Kids! Dinner's ready!" called May's mother.

"Coming, mum!" May said and flung herself off the bed.

She went over to the bathroom to wash up with her friends behind her.

As they entered the dining room, May's mother asked Ron, "Pal eats fruits, doesn't he? What all does he eat?"

"He can eat bananas and apples. He eats scrambled eggs, boiled eggs, chicken, pretty much anything, Mrs. Sparks," Said Ron, eyeing the dining table. It was full of everything. Fruit cake, tarts, pumpkin pie, pizza, salad, tomatoes and onions. There was even ice-cream for dessert!

"Ron, you know we don't eat eggs and chicken and all. We are vegetarians," Mrs. Sparks said.

"Sorry, I forgot. Anyways, I'm double hungry seeing all this food! I could eat everything here!" Ron said, happily.

"Hey! Save something for us, too!" Josh said mockingly.

They all nearly jumped onto the chairs- they were so hungry. "Yum! You cook awesome, Mrs. Sparks," Josh said in between chewing. Carra agreed. "The food's delicious!" "You should work in some kind of restaurant. It will be famous in no time! And I'll be the most frequent visitor!" Ron said, with a wide grin spreading from ear to ear.

"Kids, I don't cook so well. And I didn't cook the pizza. It's bought," Mrs. Sparks smiled. Soon, there was almost no food left on the table, but Ron was still hungry.

"Do you want more, Ron? There's more food inside," May's mother said and went inside, emerging with four bowls of noodles. She gave it to the children.

"I don't want food for a week!" Carra said, sighing.

"Wait till tomorrow morning. You won't want food for another year!" Mrs. Sparks joked.

"Oh, God," Josh groaned.

They managed to finish whatever they could and went to wash their hands. They climbed into May's bunk bed. Josh and Ron got into the lower one, which was used by May's brother who was now in England, studying college. May and Carra used the upper bunk. Near the foot of the top bunk, they had a cage installed for Snowflake. The bunny shared it with Tabitha. Pal slept on Ron, and Pete settled on a rung of the ladder.

The next day, they woke up early, which they usually don't do, since it was a Saturday. But it was the day of the pet show, and they didn't want to miss it.

"You ready, Pal?" Ron asked his dog as they went downstairs for breakfast. Pal nodded his head and they entered the dining room. A huge feast lay there, waiting. Ron's eyes widened as he surveyed the table. There was bread and butter, cheese, apple pie, veggie sandwiches, apple with custard, and a bit of yesterday night's fruit cake, pizza, and Jell-O. There was even some pieces of chocolate cake- *Chocolate Spark*, Mrs. Spark called it, her own recipe. Ron immediately sat down and gobbled it up. He was nearly done with his first round when the others came down.

"Whoa! Slow down, Ron!" May's mother said as she served a piece of apple pie for the others.

"Sorry. I was hungry," Said Ron, grinning with his mouth full. "You always are," Carra retorted as she sat down next to May. "Well, finish fast, kids. It's nearly time for the show. It's 9 o'clock. The show starts at ten, doesn't it?" May's mother asked.

"No, mom. It starts at 9:45," May answered, hurriedly gulping down her food. "Hurry, then, kids," Mrs. Sparks said and went into the kitchen.

4

The children got ready as quick as they could and were out of the door before you could say 'Cheese on marsh mellow is awful.' The four chatted as they went, with Pete sitting on Pal's head and interrupting again and again. Tabitha and Snowflake were sitting in the arms of their owners, Snowflake quietly nibbling on a carrot and Tabitha dozing. Ron kept asking Pal to perform the tricks he had taught throughout the way, to make sure he was prepared. When he wasn't doing tricks, Pal was running around, tripping everyone over.

They reached the spot of the show, which was on the grounds of an old mansion. There was a lot of place in front, where the dog show was to be held, and the cat show was to be indoors. Birds, rabbits, hamsters, guinea pigs and dogs were put on display to be adopted.

Carra went inside to put her cat in the cage to be looked at. Then she came outside to watch Pal walk around the ring. He did quite well, not even glancing at the crowd and proudly finished, wearing the medal for second place.

They all went in later to check about the cat show, and found that Tabitha had won first. Carra was beyond joy and hugged Tabitha. Ron patted her shoulder. "Good work, cousin," He said. May stroked Tabitha and the cat purred.

"I thought you didn't like the fact that we are cousins," Carra joked. "Yeah I do. But that doesn't mean I shouldn't congratulate you. I mean, Tabitha. Like, seriously, why the heck should I congratulate you?" He said. Then, seeing the look Carra gave him, he howled and ran away with Carra hot on his heels. Pal thought that was fun and ran alongside Ron, and would have lost his ribbon if Josh hadn't caught it flying in the air.

"I don't believe how careless Ron and Pal can be. Really! He nearly lost his second place ribbon! Doesn't Ron even care about that?" Josh asked May. May shrugged and turned to glimpse Carra chasing a golden tail. "I do!" came a shout from the crowd. It was Ron. He appeared suddenly, out of nowhere and snatched his ribbon. He swiftly pinned it on Pal's collar and started running, but Carra caught him. "Too slow!" Carra snickered. "Way too slow," May added. "I'm not!" Ron whimpered as he struggled in his cousin's clutches. Carra finally let go of Ron. He grunted as he smoothed down his shirt. "Look what you've done, now," He grumbled. "Like you care. You never do," He rolled his eyes at Carra and walked away with Pal alongside him, his tail up and wagging.

"Hey! Look! It's Helen! I never knew she'd come here!" Josh suddenly cried out.

"Hey, Helen!" May shouted, as she ran across the field to catch up to Helen. She was on a pony, and the owner walked away, leading the animal behind him. May stopped, out of breath. Josh had over taken her, being quite fast, but he too, stopped, and the others came to a halt beside May. Helen didn't hear them, and she and the pony were led away. "Bad luck, eh mate? Get the treasure next time, aye? Don't lose it!" Pete squawked. "Shut up, Pete," Josh said. "You've gotta learn to listen to the captain, mate. Don't fail next time. Squawk!" Pete screeched and flew away before Josh could get him.

"Will he come back?" Carra asked, unconcerned and quite relieved that Pete wasn't there to bother them.

"Yeah. Who is there out in this huge world to feed him cracker biscuits? They'll usually just shoo him away or pluck him for parrot pie,"

"What! Aren't you even a teensy bit concerned about him?" May asked, shocked.

He'll come back, don't worry. He's a smart parrot, though he is very much annoying," Josh assured her. Even as he was saying it, Pete came back.

"See? Told you!"

"Yeah, yeah. Whatever,"

They walked back to May's house, receiving a few compliments and congratulations for Tabitha and Pal. May's mother was very happy and rewarded the two animals with a whole cupcake and a biscuit each. Then she gave one cupcake to everyone else too. Pete immediately gobbled up his cupcake, dropping crumbs everywhere on the floor. Snowflake and the kids ate slowly. Everyone except Ron, that is. He gobbled up his cupcake too, like Pete.

They played games and enjoyed themselves to the core. Around 6:00 they had to go back to their own houses. They waved good bye and walked away. May sighed. She wished she could spend more time with her friends.

They met again on Sunday with Helen, and they talked for a while. Helen completely loved Pal, especially his silly nature, and couldn't stop stroking his velvety ears. Tabitha, feeling left out of the scene, went up to Helen, purring, and nuzzled her. Helen cuddled her too, and they talked about their hobbies and likes and dislikes, and thoroughly enjoyed their time together. Helen told a whole stream of jokes, and made them laugh so hard that they got a stitch in their sides.

"Okay, listen to this one- two guys were talking after their English exam. One told that he didn't get the answer to the fourth question. He said 'it was given that I should write the past tense of 'think'. I thought and thought and thought and finally wrote thinked'!" she said. Everyone burst out laughing. She told many more such jokes and burdened them with riddles.

Josh suddenly realized that he had a function to attend afterwards, and he dashed home, saying a hurried good bye to his friends, with Pete flapping his wings crazily behind him.

***

The news came with a shock. Ron discovered it and called Josh at 8:00 when he was sure that his friend was home. Josh immediately called May and passed the message on while Ron spoke to his cousin about it. Jessica snatched the phone away from Ron as he was speaking in a whisper and his sister thought that, as usual, he was complaining about her to a friend.

"Whom are you talking to?" she demanded as she placed the phone to her ear. Carra sensed that her cousin's sister was on the phone and quickly, before Ron could say anything, she said "Hi, Jessica! How are you?"

"Oh, it's you. Hi, Carra. I'm fine. How are you?" Jessica asked, glaring at Ron.

"I'm fine, Jess. He was just telling me that Pal was acting off too much just because he won second place. He was telling in a whisper mostly because Pal's there. Right?" She said, thinking fast. "Yeah. Pal's here. Well, ok, I'll give it to Ron," She said and handed over the phone to her brother.

As soon as Jessica left the room, Ron told her: Helen's name wasn't there at all in the new version of the phone book. "I just wanted to check where Helen lives, and when I checked, her name's not in the phone book. The only Baxter family here are the postman's family. You know, Peter Baxter, his wife, Ellina Baxter and their kids, Katie and Julia. No Helen Baxter here. She can't live out of town, this town's too huge and the school's plop in the middle. She said fifteen minutes away from school, but fifteen minutes away will still be in town, won't it?" he asked.

"It will. Hmm... This is quite a mystery. D'you think she lives in the forest?" Carra joked.

"Hey, wait. That could be just it! The forest is fifteen minutes away!" Ron exclaimed.

"Are you crazy or what! I was just joking! What kind of mad man lives in the forest?" Carra said and rolled her eyes all the way to the ceiling at Ron's reply.

"No really! She could live in the forest! That's why her name's not on the list! No, you've gotta believe me. It might just be true! It could be. We should check it out!" He said.

"Tomorrow. Ask May and Josh. Bye," Carra said and hung up the phone. She sighed at her cousin's stupidity.

"I already have," Ron told himself as he replaced the phone onto the table.

5

"Is it true?" May asked Josh. He shrugged. "I don't know. Ron told me so on the phone. But he didn't even explain what he was babbling about. He was much too excited to speak properly. He said he'll bring the phone book today. Beats me if he remembered,"

"He always forgets. And he forgot today, too. At least, I brought it. I knew he'd forget," Carra said walking towards them, waving a thick red book labelled 'PHONE BOOK'. She joined them, with Ron grumbling about Jessica and monsters and torture. May took the book from Carra and leafed through the book, and finally came out to 'B'. There was only Peter Baxter's family. Then she tried 'H', but obviously, to no avail. No other Baxter in town.

"Holy smokes! You're right!" Josh cried. Ron explained his theory of Helen living in the woods.

"He's crazy," Carra said, shaking her head from side to side.

"No, Carr. I think he's right!" May said, deep in thought, as she tried to work out how Helen might live in the forest.

"Only one way to find out," Josh said slyly.

"We follow her!" They said together.

***

After school, as they were waiting for Helen to finish clearing her doubts with the teacher, they talked about the phone book scheme. But, they didn't notice her coming out.

"Hi! What are you doing?" she asked as she walked over to them. "Oh, hi, Helen. We were just talking. I'd forgotten to tell you that we saw you at the pet fair. We called you, but you didn't hear. Do you have a pet?" May asked.

"Oh, sorry, I didn't hear. I thought I heard someone call me, but I thought I was just dreaming. I have- I mean, I don't have any pet. I mean I had, long ago, when I was a small girl, a Husky and a Doberman. The best companions a girl could ever have," She smiled at the memory. But it wasn't a memory. It wasn't even real. Helen never had a husky, nor did she have a Doberman. She never had any pet at all!

'Oh no. Why did I say that!' she thought, trying to keep the smile on her face.

She rescued herself by excusing herself from the group. "Sorry, I have to go. My father promised to take me to a mall today," She said. Carra tried to look jealous. "Lucky you. I have to wait a long time to go to a mall," Helen strode away, pausing to wave, and then raced off to a tall man waiting for her.

"Okay, back to business here," May said. "Look, here, everyone. Let's follow her tomorrow. We'll have to give excuses to our parents for coming home late. You two," she looked at Ron and Carra "tell your parents that you have to clean the fish tank today. Tell them you offered to do it. If that's too strange for Ron, tell your parents that Carra said that you two will do it. Okay?" They both nodded. "Josh, you tell your parents that you want to hang out with your friends in some shop. I'll tell that- wait, why not we all clean the fish tank? It's much easier that way. Okay? Got that?" Everyone nodded. "Good. Now, our parents will most likely send us extra pair of clothes for us. Let's wear something like the forest colour. Bring some black, green or brown caps as well. Wear sneakers tomorrow. After school, we follow her. Got that? Good. My mom's here, so I gotta go. Josh, please call Ron and remind him of everything, got that? Bye!" she said and ran to her black car and got in.

Carra also raced away to her bus and hopped in. She waved at the boys and she was also gone. "Umm, Josh, I nearly forgot. Mom had asked me to come with you today," Ron whimpered slowly.

"Urgghh! I could kill you!" Josh cried. Then, he calmed down. "Okay, fine. She would have called my dad, then. He'll be coming now," As soon as he said that, Josh's blue car showed up. His dad got out and waved to both of them, signalling them to come to the car.

They got in and told Josh's dad that they have to stay back in school the next day to clean the fish tank. "We can walk home, dad, or just give us some cash and we'll catch a cab home. Or we can use our own pocket money," Josh said. "Sure, son. I won't have any time tomorrow to pick you up, tomorrow. Take a bit of money from my side and enjoy yourselves. Buy some ice-cream or something," His dad said taking a right turn. Ron fell on Josh on purpose and they did that all the way to their houses even if it was a slight turn. Ron stayed at his friend's house for some time, and played a few games with him. When they were sure their other two friends had reached home, they called them to tell them about their taxi plans. The girls agreed and hung up. Ron went home and made himself a very roasted sandwich as he had absolutely no idea how to make one. It tasted so horrible that he threw it in the dustbin and ate a strawberry cupcake instead. Pal appeared on the scene and tried to knock Ron down to eat the rest of the cupcake, but was told very firmly to sit, and had no other choice but to obey. Ron decided to go for a walk in the park with Pal, and left a note for his mom, who would be back very soon. They walked over to the park where they met a poodle. Pal raced over to the poodle and sniffed her tail. They both strained on their leashes, wanting to play, but Ronald sternly told 'Sit' in a very firm voice. Pal grudgingly obeyed and the poodle and her owner walked away.

Ron sat down on a bench, and Pal grumpily flopped down beside his legs. As much as he loved his master, he felt sorry for himself. Right now, he wanted to play but was not allowed to. But just then, he sensed something. A secret! Ron, his beloved master, (whom he somewhat despised a second ago) was hiding a secret from him! He should find out what that secret is! He was suddenly very curious and looked up at the boy with questioning eyes. He opened his mouth wide, hanging his tongue out. Then he put his paws on Ron's lap, doing all he could to get the boy to talk. Ron knew at once that Pal found out that he was hiding something from his dog, and barely just managed to stifle a smile. He simply said "I can't wait till tomorrow", just to see what the retriever's reaction might be. Pal looked even more puzzled than ever. He pushed Ron's knees, and looked up beseechingly.

"All right, all right, I'll tell you!" Ron said pretending to sigh. Secretly, he was proud of his dog for being so understanding and polite. He was proud of Pal for other reasons, too.

"You know that girl, Helen, right? You've seen her many times before, haven't you?" Ron asked. Pal nodded. Ron smiled and continued. "Well, her name wasn't on the phone book, I checked. Well, we," Ron stopped and looked down at Pal to check if he understood. Pal knew that 'we' meant Ron, Josh, May and Carra. "We thought about it, and came to the-wait, what is that word? It means something like 'point'?" Ron asked Pal. "How would I know?" Pal seemed to say.

Oh, I got it! It's 'conclusion!'" Ron exclaimed. "Okay, now. Where was I?" Pal appeared to be rolling his eyes. "Oh, yeah. I remember. Yeah, well, we thought about it, talked, and maybe argued, but finally, we came to the conclusion" he highlighted that word. "That Helen might live in the forest," Ron's eyes shone with excitement. Pal hung his long tongue out even longer and panted faster. Now even he couldn't wait until the next day! They went home, and Ron told his mother grumpily that he had to stay back in school the next day. "Why? Did you do anything bad today to get detention? Didn't answer question asked by teachers? Didn't do a project? Failed in Maths test? Or any test for that matter?" his mother asked suspiciously as she washed and wiped dishes clean. "No no! It's all Carra's fault," he started, but was interrupted by his mother. "And why is it so?"

"She told Mr. Nestor that we both would stay back and clean the fish tank," He muttered.

"Hah! Serves you right, baby!" Jessica teased. She came in, flicking her long, curly, brown hair over her shoulder and took out her guitar.

"Mom! Are you free for about five to ten minutes? I've just composed this song, and I wanna show it to you."

"Sure, dear. Just a minute. I'll finish all these dishes and come up. You can be practising it. Ron, I think you should take another pair of clothes to clean the fish tank. After that, finish your homework! I'll check it after Jessie shows her song to me, got that? Go, now!" she said and shooed him out of the kitchen.

6

The four found it hard to concentrate during the classes the next day. Their minds were set in the adventure ahead of them. They kept whispering to one another, but May told them to act casual and talk to Helen normally, too, even though her own excitement threatened to give everything away.

Thankfully, Mrs. Fitch was absent since her son was not well and she had to take care of him. Mr. Leslie arrived for substitution, and he was their favourite teacher. He taught very well, and almost never gave detention.

Physics, a boring class was next, and Ron tried as hard as he could to get the teacher to explain the chapter again and again to pass time. In the end, Josh applauded him and thanked him because he had not read the chapter and was sure that the teacher would ask questions. Helen laughed too, and admitted that even she was not thorough with the lesson, and thanks to Ron's repeated efforts, she cleared her doubts.

It felt like time was playing a trick on them by going slowly, but in the end, stopped and the bell trilled. The four heaved a sigh of relief and walked out as fast as they could.

They had decided to do some tank cleaning because none of them liked to lie to their parents. They also asked Helen to join them so that it would be easier to follow her later on. So they quickly changed in their respective rooms, and met in the biology room where the tanks were kept.

They cleaned the tank up a bit, by putting the fish in a bucket full of water. They put the fish back inside the cleaned tank and walked out, talking to each other. Josh and Ron told them that they needed to go home, and they both went away, leaving May and Carra with Helen. But instead of staying home, Josh and Ron snuck into each of the four houses and stole away with the four animals. They hid the animals in the forest, told them to stay put, and then raced back to a shortcut to the forest. Meanwhile, as May and Carra were talking with Helen, May casually asked, "Where do you live? We would love to see your house," But Helen politely refused. Helen then left May and Carra. They noticed that Helen wasn't actually going in the direction of the forest, but still, they met up with the boys in the shortcut and reached the forest. There, to their surprise, they spotted her entering the forest.

"See? Told you! I was right!" Ron exclaimed and stuck out his tongue at Carra. "Ron, that's not a very nice thing to do," May said, disgusted.

"Whatever," He said and crept after Helen. The others, trying their best not to be noticed, joined him to see where she had gone. She had stopped beside an oak tree.

They wondered what she was doing there, but Josh was more worried about his parrot. Pete was hidden between the oak leaves, where Josh had put him earlier, and he was going to fly down and give them away! But it seemed that she already knew they were there.

"It is a great place, right?" she asked. Then she tilted her head backwards, and, digging out some cashews from inside her pocket, called, "Come, down, Pete. Your name is Pete, correct?" she asked. Pete, for now, was camouflaged, but was coming out since he got an invitation. He was an animal of action, and he didn't need to be told twice if someone was holding out food for him.

Josh murmured softly, "Please don't come out," But Pete couldn't hear that, and flew down and gobbled up the food held in Helen's hand. Josh smacked his head with his hand.

"You can come out. I know you are hiding," She said, and paused. When they didn't come out, she continued, "Behind the bushes,"

"How did you know?!" Ron asked, shocked. He jumped out, followed by Pal. May came out next, followed by her friends.

"Do you live here?" Carra asked, shocked.

"What is your problem if I live here or not?" Helen asked a little annoyed.

"Why can't I ask?" Carra asked feeling irritated.

"Guys," May said. "Helen, you have a beautiful house, that is, if you live here". Helen didn't answer.

"Do you live in a tree house or something?" Ron asked, mystified.

"Ron," May said.

"No, I mean it. Do you-,"

"Ron. Don't blabber," May said.

"I wasn't!"

"Are you our friend?" Josh asked the first question that came to his head to stop Ron from continuing.

"Yes. Kind of," Helen said.

"What do you mean, kind of?" Josh asked.

"Well, you followed me, so I do not think of you as my friend. But since you are kind to me, I say it is only fair that you all are my friends,"

"Okaaay," May said. She lifted an eyebrow.

"What?" Helen asked.

"That means she wants an explanation," Carra explained.

"Explanation of what?"

"What you are doing here."

"What will I be doing here? I'm going to my house that is all," Helen said, then clamped her hands over her mouth.

"Aha! The truth is out! You've spilt the beans!" May cheered.

"What do you mean? I do not have any beans with me," Helen said, wondering.

"It's an idiom," May explained.

"What is an idiom?"

"It's just a phrase. The bean is the truth. So, you've spilt the truth. There are many phrases like that," Josh said.

"You said you live here?" Ron asked, trying to change the subject.

"Yes, I do," Helen said.

"What do you eat?" Ron asked.

"I was expecting that question from you," Carra joked. Ron rolled his eyes all the way to the sky. He looked back at Helen.

"Fruits, vegetables," She answered.

"How do you live?" Ron asked.

"What do you mean?" She asked.

"What do you do in your home?"

"I guard the borders, I learn, and I play," She said without thinking.

"You guard!" May cried, shocked.

"Whoops," Helen said softly. Then she said louder, "Okay, here goes nothing. Listen, I know that you are all shocked. But I have given away too many secrets which human kind should not know. I cannot-,"

"Whoa, whoa, whoa! What do you mean, 'human kind should not know'! Aren't you a human?" Josh interrupted.

"No,"

"Then what the heck are you?" Ron exclaimed.

"I cannot tell."

"At least tell this- how long have you been living here?"

"More than three-fourth of my whole life of one thousand seven hundred and forty- nine," She said, amused.

"What!" The four of them cried together.

"Tough to take in, is it not?" she asked, grinning.

"You are certainly so un-human!" Ron said, a bit scared. Pal, who sensed that Ron was frightened a bit, growled at Helen, knowing that she was the reason that Ron was scared.

Suddenly, he turned tail and fled behind a bush, dragging Ron by his jeans. It was a total mayhem. Two white tigers had appeared out of nowhere, and they were the reason Pal had shot off like that. Pete started squawking uncontrollably. May and Carra shrieked and rushed off to the bush where Snowflake was. Josh climbed up a tree and sat next to Tabitha there. Pete also came up and sat on Josh's brown hair. Only Helen didn't get frightened and just stood there, in front of the tigers.

"What the heck! Helen, come here! You'll get hurt!" May cried.

But mysteriously, the tigers didn't attack! One just sat and the other climbed onto the first one's back. Helen just stood there, watching. She waited until the tigers had finished rolling over in the mud, then she spoke.

"Victoria, Ivy, will you stop?"

The tigers stopped playing and both sat up straight.

"What the heck's she doing?" May hissed.

"Talking to tigers. Duh," Carra said. They looked back at Helen.

"Ivy, you know better than that," She was saying.

Then, an amazing thing happened. One of the tigers talked! Ron nearly fainted.

"Even you should know better than pulling everyone into camp," It said. "You know Father will be mad. You are going to be in very big trouble," It lay down and basked in the sun. The other decided to give itself a wash, and began talking as well. Now, Ron really did faint, but only momentarily. He came to, pretty soon.

"Do you think Ruben would mind this?" the tiger washing itself asked the other one. "I do not know," It replied.

"Ivy," Helen said and walked over to the one sleeping. She coaxed it to get up, until, finally, she managed to succeed. "I did not ask them to come. Is it my fault that they followed me here?" she asked.

"Yes, in a way. And this is exactly why you should not go to school. Quit it," The tiger said simply and yawned.

Josh, who was a brave boy, climbed down the tree and walked over to the tigers and Helen.

"So, you can talk?" he asked cautiously.

"Could you not hear us, boy? If you did, and I am most certain you did, you would know by now," The one which was washing itself, named Victoria said.

The other one, Ivy trotted over to Josh and sniffed him. He stood still, trying to act cool, but shaking with fear.

May managed to gather her wits and strolled out from behind the bush. Victoria immediately came running to sniff her. May jumped back in fear, but Victoria could easily get to her again. But she stopped when Helen yelled at her and Ivy to stop. They both retreated back to Helen. Suddenly, Ivy transformed into a girl!

May shrieked in surprise and shock, and Josh too took a step or two backwards.

The girl looked a bit older than them, and surprisingly, had the same eyes, hair and face of Helen.

"Ron, Carra, you can come out," Helen called. "This is my sister, Ivy,"

"That's your sister?" Carra cried. "But she was a tiger! And now she's a human! And she looks like she's gonna eat you!"

Helen laughed. "I will explain everything to you if you settle down and Ronald comes out," Helen said.

"Hey, Josh! Get him out, will you, please?" Carra shouted.

"Yeah, wait," He ran to the bush which was shaking the most, because Ron was trembling so much. "Hey, man, get out. They won't do anything," He kept at it, but when Ron didn't come, he tried coaxing Pal. "Pal, come on, boy, please. They won't hurt you, I promise," He persuaded Pal again and again, until, finally, Pal believed him and dragged a shouting and kicking Ron out of the bush.

"Good boy," Josh praised and walked away.

"BAD BOY!" Ron screamed. As soon as he said that, Pal dropped his leg and made the puppy face at Ron. He knew that Ron couldn't resist that face and would forgive him. He was right.

"All right. Come on," Ron grumbled. He walked towards Josh with Pal trotting alongside him.

"Here, sit on this," Victoria, still a tiger, shoved a log towards them. Tabitha, Snowflake and Pete had come out by now.

"Vic," Ivy said.

"Take it easy, Ivy," Victoria said, looking at her. Unusually, Victoria's eyes were also green.

"It's okay," Helen said. "They won't give anything away,"

"How are you so sure?" Ivy glared at her.

"Ask them," Helen shrugged.

"Iris. Can I talk to you for a minute?" Ivy asked.

"Who's Iris?" May asked. Helen just said "I will tell you later," Then she and her sister vanished behind the trees and bushes.

"Why have you come here?" Victoria asked, calmly washing her face.

"I'm still not used to talking with a tiger," Ron whimpered.

Victoria laughed. "That is perfectly okay. No one ever is brave enough to come out like that. They would rather just faint,"

"But I did," Ron mumbled.

"Well, I'm fine enough with talking to you, as long as you don't eat me up," Josh said, sitting on the log.

"No, no, we do not eat humans," Victoria laughed again. She walked over and sat in front of the log.

"Come, have a seat," She offered. May sat on the log, followed by Carra. But Ron was still not convinced. He stood away from Victoria, not trusting the tiger's word. Tabitha walked over to Victoria and sniffed her.

"What is your name?" asked Victoria.

Tabitha, taken by surprise, shot back and hid behind Carra.

"I am sorry. I had forgotten that they do not speak," Victoria apologized.

"No, no, it's perfectly all right," Carra said.

"How is it that you can talk?" May burst out. She couldn't hold that question back any longer.

"Iris will explain that to you later,"

"Who's Iris?" Ron asked. He was becoming interested now. He came over and sat next to Josh. Pal sat by his feet.

Victoria looked shocked. "She is Ivy's sister. You are friends with her!" she said.

"You mean Helen?" Carra asked.

"Yes. She has taken that name. I had forgotten,"

7

"Your name is Iris? How come you said your name is Helen?" May said.

"I know. I could not tell you my real name because that would be a crime," Iris said.

"But Hel-I mean Ivy, sorry, I meant Iris, but..," Carra's voice trailed off.

"You said you lived in some Crowfield," May said.

"Yes, I did. I mean I said I did. But I just said that because I'm not allowed to tell anyone about all this right?" Iris grinned.

"Yeah.. How does that shape-shifting thingy happen?" May wanted to know.

"I am not very good at this. So I will give the job of explaining about ourselves to Ivy," Iris grinned. Ivy opened her mouth to protest but Victoria cut her off.

"You will have to explain it, Ivy. Iris is not good at it,"

"There is something you must know about us, but you will have to keep it as a secret. Iris, show it," Ivy nodded at her sister. Everyone looked at Iris.

Iris suddenly vanished and a horse stood in her place. Before anyone could react, Ivy said, "That is our speciality. We can transform into any animal we want,"

Then Iris came back to her own self. "So that's why you were a tiger just now!" Carra exclaimed. Ivy nodded.

"Technically, not just now, but-" Ron started but Josh cut him off. "Shut up, Ron," He said.

"You understand fast. I did not get any of your names. Please tell their names too," Ivy pointed at their pets.

"I'm May. She's Carra and that's her cousin Ronald. He's Josh. That's Snowflake, my bunny, he's Pal, Ron's dog, that's Tabitha, Carra's cat, and that's Josh's parrot, Pete over there," May said.

"Ah," Victoria said.

"So, as I said, we can transform into an animal and I.. Umm, I, it is actually a bit tough to explain it. See, it is very complicated," Ivy said.

"Whatever," Josh shrugged.

"Ivy? They seem really interested. Do you think..?" Victoria said, talking as if the four weren't even there.

"In fact, yes, we are very interested," May, said, delighted.

Ivy looked at Iris and Victoria. Iris looked pleading. Ivy took a deep breath. "Please excuse me," She said and plopped down, all the way down to the ground, as a little monkey. She rubbed her eyes with her little paws, and shook her tail.

Then, she looked up with beady little eyes. She scanned the trees, and became a human again.

"I am - I'm sorry about that," Ivy said. "It helps me, umm, control myself. I, I sometimes lose myself,"

"Nah. It's no problem at all," Ron said carelessly. He eagerly waited for Ivy to continue.

"Our- what do you call that- our clan, you can say, we are called Ronens. We are somehow interconnected to the animals here. Long ago, we came from another planet. Our bonds were different back then, in the shapes of animals over there. But life here has altered their genes and caused them to take the forms of Earth's animals permanently. Life as a Ronen runs on a daily basis. Youngsters learn the rules and terms and the important biological lessons by the teachers. They are given an adult to be taught how to hunt and fight against our enemies. That adult teaches the youngster until that Ronen is 2,500 years old. Then, it is like becoming 25 years in human age. They start training when they are 500 years. We grow very slowly. Only Leif has completed his training," Ivy explained.

"Who's Leif?" Josh asked.

"He is our elder brother," Iris said.

"You have a brother?" May asked.

"Yes. And another sister, too," Ivy added.

"Her name is Lily," Iris said.

"Is she elder than you?" Carra asked. Ivy laughed. "No, she is the youngest of our family. She started her training recently. She is around 850 years old,"

"Eight hundred and thirty- three years, to be exact," Iris said. They both smiled at the same time. They looked a lot like each other.

"One minute. Do you have to study anything? You said teachers are going to teach something?" Ron started turning pale.

"Yes, you have to study biology," Iris grinned. Ivy didn't understand why Ron looked so shocked, so her sister explained it to her. "He barely passes biology tests,"

Ivy laughed. "That's ok. Even I failed first time,"

"You did?!" May exclaimed. She was very good in bio.

Victoria yawned. "I am feeling sleepy, Ivy. I am going back home. Are you coming?"

"I'll come. So, what is your plan? I feel you are desperate to live with us and see our ways?" Ivy asked.

"We are, but... what do we tell our parents?"Josh asked. "Come back tomorrow. We would have told Father by then, and we can come to your houses to convince your parents to join us," Ivy reassured him.

That day, the four narrated the whole incident to their parents. Of course, nobody believed them. The next day Iris and Ivy brought along some older Ronens to talk to the parents. They narrated their history and demonstrated their special skills. The Ronens were preparing for a fight against their enemies, and they needed more manpower. They were only happy to welcome the children and their family to their clan. May and her friends were too eager for this adventure and pleaded with their parents to let them go. However, it was hard to convince the parents and only May's mother seemed to believe them; they did not want to send their children with some strange people, to some strange land. Eventually, the parents gave in. after a long discussion, it was decided that children could join the Ronens and they would be accompanied by one parent each. May's mother, Carra's father, Ron's mother and Josh's father decided to go with the children.

8

The night before the departure, the children were very excited. Carra had a strange feeling that they may never return, which made her think about her friends and school. She was also wondering about what type of clothes will be suitable for this new place they were going to. So she asked her mother whether she could take her miniskirts. Carra's mother, who was getting a bit apprehensive about this sudden turn of events and the journey ahead of them, did not pay much attention to her daughter's wardrobe concerns. Josh was thinking if he should take Pete's cage. His dad solved his problem. "You are going to the wild, Josh. Why need a cage there?" He asked. Josh nodded.

Soon, all the four families were ready. They slept early and woke up at five-thirty. The clan was going to move to another forest at seven thirty, and they had to reach there before six. They got ready as quickly as they could. They reached the edge of the forest and found Ivy, Iris, Victoria and a huge hawk waiting for them.

"Hello," Iris greeted them. "This is Ruben," She said, gesturing at the hawk. "Hello. Iris has told me a lot about you four," Ruben said.

"Come, let us go. It is nearly time for us to leave," Ivy said.

"Why are you leaving again?" Josh's father asked.

"We got to know that the forest is going to be cleared," Iris said. Ivy started giving orders. "Victoria, carry Josh and his father. Ruben, you take Ron and his mother with the dog. Iris you take Carra and her father with Tabitha and I'll take Mrs Sparks and May," she said. Then, she transformed into a huge lion and stood patiently. Iris turned into a giant eagle and beckoned to Carra to get on her back. Carra picked up Tabitha and walked over to the eagle. She placed her cat onto Iris and climbed up. Her parents followed her. The others also climbed up Ivy, Ruben and Victoria. But when Iris was just about to take off, Tabitha started squirming. She did *not* want to sit on a giant eagle, and she wanted to make sure everyone knew that.

"Oh no. I wish I'd brought her cage," Carra sighed.

"Don't worry, Carra," Her father laughed. "I had packed it," He reached into one of their two luggage bags and pulled out a bright pink and blue cage. "Oh, thank you, dad," She opened the door of the cage and put the white cat inside.

"I will carry her with my claws. There will be more place for you and your luggage then," Iris said. Carra climbed down and placed Tabitha's cage near Iris' talons. Then she climbed onto her back again. "Ok," She said. When Iris lifted her wings, Tabitha started yowling loudly, fearing that they might leave her and go away. But she stopped as soon as Iris lifted her cage. She settled down and kept quiet. Iris scanned the area as she waited for Ruben to come up.

"How far away is your home from here?" Ron asked. "It is 20 minutes from here," Victoria answered. "Then Pal can run behind us. He certainly can't fit here," He said. "Will you do that, Pal?" He asked his dog. Pal barked, agreeing with his master, and he sat down, not wanting to waste any energy at the moment. Pete was going to fly, and Snowflake was sitting on May's lap. Josh and his dad quickly sat on the hawk, and Ruben lifted his mighty wings. He flapped and reached Iris. They called out to Ivy that they will go to the camp, and then, they flew. They went quite fast, but the ride was smooth. Pete had to rest for some time; the other two birds went too fast for a parrot.

In the middle, Iris stopped abruptly. Carra fell on her giant neck. "What happened, Iris?" she asked. "What's wrong?"

"Nothing. Lily. Oh, why can't she just stay in camp! Why does she always run away?" She muttered to herself and swooped down, with Ruben hot on her tail. They touched the ground, and as soon as they all got off, Iris changed back into a girl and Ruben shrank until he was the size of a normal hawk.

Iris picked up a little mouse scurrying along the path. As soon as she picked it up, Victoria and Ivy came. "Let me down!" The mouse squeaked. The four friend's parents were shocked. But Ron, Josh, May and Carra were used to this now. "Who's that?" Josh asked. "This is Lily, my sister," Ivy said. "Your sister is a... mouse?" Ron's mother asked uncertainly. "No," Iris laughed. "She is a girl, only in the form of a mouse," She let the mouse down, and it became a young, beautiful girl. "Where were you going off to, huh? You are supposed to stay in camp!" Iris scolded. She turned to her friends.

"This is Lily. Say hi," Iris said. "Hi," Lily said shyly and hid behind her sister. "Lily," Ivy said. She went behind Iris and tickled the girl. "Where is Misty?" she asked.

"Who's Misty?" Josh asked. "Everyone around here have a special connection with one animal. That animal and person will bond and then, risk their lives for each other. They usually are together Iris and I are bonds," Ruben explained. "So that's why I sawa hawk every day in school after Iris joined!" Ron exclaimed.

"Yes, that was me. And I saw you four too, every day." Ron looked at Josh in contempt, who rolled his eyes and said, "Okay, you were right. For once,"

"How do you bond?" Carra asked. "We promise each other that we will be there for each other in an oath," Ivy said. She hesitated, for a minute. "Well, what is the oath?" May asked.

"It goes like this-

We shall protect each other until death,

And never abandon each other,

I pledge that we will be together,

And so shall rest as bonds," She recited.

"Ah," Ron's mother said.

"So Ruben is your bond, and Victoria is Ivy's bond. Right?" Josh asked. "Yes," Ivy answered for Iris. "And Misty's Lily's bond, right?" Carra asked. "Yes," Ivy answered again. There was a loud swoosh, and then, as a bat landed, it shrank in size. "So, this is Misty, if I'm not wrong," May said. "You are not wrong. This is Misty, Lily's bond," Iris said. Tabitha, who was out of her cage, went over and sniffed the bat. But she didn't like the smell of Misty, so she turned away with her tail high up in the air, looking as proud as the ruler of the world would be, and walked back towards Carra. Misty, outraged at this display of a cat, which she actually considered as a very low species of animals, flew to Tabitha, screeching, and sat on the cat, clawing her precious collar. The cat, angered at the thought of a much damaged pink collar, (Which she prized as how a man would prize a collection of diamonds) tried to roll over, in an attempt to squish Misty, but she flew away in time. But that didn't stop her, and she flew back screeching and clawing. Tabitha in turn, was trying to claw and bite the little bat. They didn't stop fighting until Ruben came over (very soon, though) and gripped Misty's wings in his claws. Tabitha was still hissing and it took her a moment or two to relax. She calmed down and sat in her cage. Ruben came down and let go of Misty. The little bat flapped over to Lily. She made herself bigger, and Lily sat on her back. She hissed at Tabitha before they flew away, but the cat did not notice. The rest continued their journey. They reached pretty soon, with Ruben reaching the camp first, since he was the strongest of the four. It started drizzling just then, and all except Pal hurried to Iris's father's cave. "Pal! Come here!"Ron called. Pal sneaked one regretful look at the sky, and bounded over to the cave. Once inside, he immediately shook his fur, splattering all of them with water. "Pal!" May and Carra screeched. Pal looked at them wearing the puppy face expression, and they immediately smiled. No matter what this dog did, one look at that puppy face, and they had to forgive him. They couldn't resist!

"Father! We have brought our friends!" Ivy called. A lot of rumbling, shaking, and moaning could be heard. When all of them thought a monster, or maybe a dragon would emerge from the darkness, out popped a little grey squirrel.

"Ahem! Sorry," The squirrel apologized.It started growing huger and huger, transforming into a man.The four friends were astonished. The man had brown hair and stunning green eyes, much like his three daughters.

"Hello," the man smiled. "I am Iris's father. Call me Avaron," He turned to the cave and called, "Chester! Go and call Minkin, will you, please?" "I will!" a deep voice answered. A lion came padding out. The four friend's parents were shocked, but May, Carra, Josh and Ron were used to this, too. "This is Chester," Avaron said, gesturing towards the lion. "Chester, these are their friends. They will join our clan," "Hello," The lion purred. "This is May, Carra, Ron and Josh," Ivy said. They smiled at the lion. She introduced the pets to Chester. Tabitha, for one, seemed extremely irritated to meet him. She growled and walked away to Victoria.

Chester raced away and came back five minutes later, a bit damp, with a man and wolf on either side of him. The rain then stopped, and the clouds moved to give way for bright sunlight.

"This is Minkin. After your ritual is over, Ivy and Iris will show you everyone in this clan," Avaron introduced.

"What ritual?" Carra asked curiously.

"Do not worry. It is a simple practice which you will need to undergo to become an official member of the clan," Avaron assured her.

"Come. Let us not waste any time," Minkin said. "Jasper, please fetch the required materials for me," Minkin asked. "Yes. One minute," The wolf said and dashed away. He was back in two minutes, clutching a few things in his mouth. He kept it down on the ground and began to arrange the wood pieces he had brought with him. Minkin took out some fruits from a basket and arranged them around the wood pieces. Then they set the wood on fire. After five minutes, they called four people to sit around the blazing fire.

"We can do it only four at a time," Minkin said. "Let the kids go first. We'll go later," The parents decided.

The four friends sat around the fire.

"Please sit still for now. Later, you will have to do exactly as I tell you. Do you understand?" Minkin asked this question in such a way that the kids felt that it was their duty to say 'I do.'

He started the ritual by chanting something from a book. Then, he took out some water from a pot and sprinkled it over them. Then, he put his hand into the fire, still chanting, and took out a handful of flames in his hand! Ron squealed. He then threw the flames on the children! But none of the flames even touched a single hair on even one of them. The fire simply died away. May glanced at her mother, who looked distraught. She mouthed the words 'I'm okay' at her mother and turned her attention back to Minkin. He was deep inside his book, but turned to them soon.

"Now, look here carefully. Each of you will have to walk through the fire. It will purify your soul and help you become one of us. After walking through the fire, lie down on that patch of salt there," he pointed at a huge pile near the wall of the cave to show them where it was, "for about five minutes, then go to the lake and bathe. Ivy and Iris will show you where the lake is located," He instructed. Ivy and Iris nodded. "Who wants to go first?" Minkin asked. "I will," Certainly, as everyone expected, the bravest of them all, Josh had agreed to go first. His father looked proud, but little nervous.

"You are Jo-Josh, right?" The priest asked, frowning at his book. "Yeah," He said, looking at the fire. "Just walk straight in. Stand in the middle of the fire, for about two or three seconds. Then lie down in the salt, on your back for two minutes, then on your stomach for two minutes. Then bathe. Did you get that?" Minkin asked, looking him squarely in the eye. "Yes," Josh said, looking him truthfully in the eyes. The priest studied him for a moment, and then said "Good. You may proceed," He gestured to the fire. Josh nodded and walked straight in with no fear. He trusted this Minkin, even though he barely knew him, and knew that this priest would not let him burn up. He waited for two seconds before moving on. He did feel some burning sensation on his skin, but as soon as he stepped out, it extinguished. Pete was screeching uncontrollably. He had thought that Josh was going to burn up in the fire. But when Josh stepped out, he stopped his noise and flew to Josh. Ruben quickly caught him. No one should disturb the people undergoing the ritual. After striding out, Josh immediately lay down on the salt on his back. After five minutes, Iris led him to a lake and May stepped into the fire. Just as he came back, drenched from head to toe, May stood up and followed Ivy to the lake. Iris pointed to an empty cave, on the other side of the clearing, and Josh's father immediately shuffled him there to wipe him clean. When he came out of the cave, May was returning, also dripping. Ron was leaving for the lake with Iris. Josh and his father walked out as May and her mother stepped in.

After everyone finished, the parents sat around the fire. The ritual for the parents was different. Meanwhile, the sisters took the four friends around the camp, introducing Ronens to them.

9

They chatted together as they walked back to the camp. The four found out more and more about Iris and her clan. They ate fruits. On the planet from where they came, they used to eat a little pink plant with blue and green flowers called Frex. They had hunters who hunted and fought, teachers who taught, weavers who wove, doctors who healed and watchers who guarded the camp day and night. They all had come from another planet, whose name the sisters refused to tell, for some unknown reason. The Ronens were driven out from their whole planet by evil forces. A battle had been fought, and Leif too had participated, but the three sisters were too young. Lily was extremely young, just around 200 to 300 years old.

When they reached camp, animals and Ronens alike were scurrying along, packing. The hunters and their bonds brought more and more food. The weaver's bonds were running everywhere, packing warm blankets and clothes for everyone while their bonds stitched on. The doctors and their bonds packed bottles and bottles of medicine and other necessary items they needed. The teachers were carefully packing their own bags. A boy a little elder than Lily came running up to them.

"Hello!" He said cheerfully. "Hello, Haze," Iris said, ruffling his hair. "This is Haze. He is my father's brother's son. He has a twin sister. Her name is Hazel," She pointed at a girl with a jaguar. Then she pointed at an eagle. "She is Jewel. She is Haze's bond,"

"Ah..," Carra said.

"I noticed that all you Ronens have green eyes. If we become Ronens, will our eyes become green too?" May asked.

"I doubt so. Check your mother's eyes, May,"

"Why do you doubt it?" Carra asked.

"All Ronens who are born as Ronens have green eyes. But till now, no one but one has ever joined our clan. But the man who had joined already had green eyes."

"Who is that?" Ron asked.

"Father."

"Wait, what?! How come!??"

Iris simply chuckled. "Father joined long ago. He was from another clan, the Eyrons. He had strayed too far from his own clan, with his mother, and was lost. But then, after a short time, even he and his mother were separated. The Ronen leader then had found him, and by the time they could send him back to their own clan, he had learnt too much of the Ronens. So, they had to permit him to stay. Minkin had helped in the ritual; he was also only Father's age then," Ivy explained.

"Then how is he the leader of your clan?"

"He was a born hunter, he gained everyone's respect and they elected him as the leader,"

"How does that happen? Voting or what?"

"Not precisely. The leader first shortlists a few names, and those selected Ronens will stand aside. Then, a vote is cast by the rest, and those who were selected do not vote. The top three who gets the majority votes will go through a series of tests. They all are sent to spy on their enemies to test them. They are sent to battle with dangerous creatures, but the other Ronens make sure none of them are seriously injured. Then, they have to organize battles and their knowledge at basic medicine is tested," Ivy said.

"And your father was selected?"

"Yes. But, they shouldn't just outlive these qualities; they have to gain the trust from the Ronens too," Iris added.

"That means you're all only half Ronen and half something else?" Josh asked.

"Yes, I suppose so. But Lily does not know it yet, so we had better keep it that way," Ivy added.

"Would Pal, Pete, Snowflake and Tabitha's thing be over now?" Ron suddenly asked.

They had left their pets behind with their parents for the ritual.

"Most probably," Ivy said. Iris shrugged.

"Let's go check it," Carra suggested.

The six friends trudged back to the mouth of Avaron's cave, where the ritual was held. Minkin was telling Snowflake to do something.

"Carra!" A voice which they had never heard before, but closely resembled Tabitha's voice, shrieked. They whirled around and Tabitha came running up to them purring as loudly as she could. "There are so many things I need to tell you! The first thing-" She was interrupted by a little louder, more doggish and growlish voice.

"Rrrooonnn!" It shouted joyfully as Pal came bouncing up to Ron and knocked him over.

"Pal!" Ron shouted too, and they both laughed. Tabitha looked at Pal in annoyance. She hissed at him, too, but he didn't seem to notice. Even if he had, he didn't bother to do anything to the cat. He was much too busy trying to lick Ron.

"Get off, boy!" Ron laughed, shoving the dog away.

"I can taaalk!" Pal barked loudly and ran around crazily.

"Pal, stop that," May said, giggling.

"Maaay!" He said, and then stopped. "Maay. No, Maay," He looked confused.

"It's May. With one little 'a'. Just one," May smiled.

"May," Pal said. Then he looked hopefully at her. "Did I get it right?"

"Yes," She chuckled.

"He may have a little problem talking, but with a little guidance from someone, he will soon perfect the art of speaking," Minkin said, walking over. "He didn't pay enough attention during the ritual. This is an effect of his distracted nature. And you four, you will have to repeat your process. It has quiet not been done, it seems. You may do the ritual to become bonds, but you all are not officially Ronens yet. Do you understand?" He asked. They all nodded sincerely, and Ron frowned at Pal. "Pal," He said, trying to sound like he was a person of great authority. Pal just did the puppy face and everything was settled.

Pal then noticed Josh and Carra. "Jooshh! Carrrraa!" He barked joyfully. He waited for them to correct him. "It's Josh, Pal. One 'o' and one 'h'. Ok?" Josh said.

"Jo - Joosh. Noo, wait. It is... Josh," He tried hard, twisting his mouth, trying to get it right.

"Yes! Well done, Pal!" Ron cheered, forgetting his anger.

"He may not be a good speaker, but he has a lot of enthusiasm. He will learn fast," Minkin approved.

"Caara?" He asked hopefully.

"Good try," Carra patted his head. "You've just interchanged it. There's two 'r's and one 'a'. 'K?" She smiled at him. He tried again, now getting it right. "Good boy!" Ron said proudly.

Tabitha was getting tired of everyone praising only Pal. *She* was the one who needed attention, not Pal. She walked to the centre and purred loudly, with her tail held high. She ignored Pal, and addressed them loudly.

"Carra, I have longed to talk to you from when I was a little kitty. Firstly, I want to thank you- Silence!" She hissed at Pal, who sniffed, and continued, "I want to thank you for rescuing me and sheltering me. Second, I am indebted to you for showering endless love and care on me. And certainly, not to miss out, shelter, food and warmth. Without you, I wouldn't have made it to this age of 2 and half years. Thank you," She said to the audience, then walked over to Carra proudly.

"Aww," May said, clapping. Ivy and her sister were impressed. Ron and Josh clapped too. Even Pal barked "Nice speeech!"

"Thank you," Tabitha mewed shyly to Pal. "It's just 'speech', Pal, not 'speeech'," Carra said. "And thanks, Tabby," She smiled tenderly at her cat, carrying her and scratching her behind her ears.

"Josh!!!" Came a voice. "Well, the party's arrived. No one can miss out the parrot!" Josh grinned. "Pete!" he called happily. Pete flew over and spread his wings over Josh's neck, like hugging him. Josh laughed and hugged him too.

"I can speak things other than pirate things now!" he squawked happily. But before he could get anything else out-

"Herbulen!" a loud voice roared. Pal immediately flopped to the ground, with his rump standing, his paws over his eyes.

"Don't worry. It is only Chester. You remember him, do you not? He was just calling the doctor," Iris asked them.

"Chester's your father's bond, right?"

"Yes, he is,"

"Don't we have to bond too?" Ron asked, rubbing Pal's tummy, whose tongue was licking the floor in the silliest manner.

"Of course. Everyone needs a bond. There are some other lone animals whom I know who your parents can bond," Iris said. She led them back to the ritual site. Minkin was waiting for them there.

"You have come for the bonding, I believe," He said, sitting down. The fire was still blazing.

"Yes. We both have to get something. We will be right back," Iris said and she ran away with her sister.

"The four sat down with their pets by their sides. Snowflake, who had just finished her ritual, was sitting so silently that they thought that she could not speak and the ritual had failed for her. Then finally,

"Snowflake, are you feeling all right?" May asked.

Snowflake opened her mouth to squeak, but instead found herself speaking the same language as May!

"I- I can talk!" she stammered.

"Welcome to the new world," Ron rolled his eyes.

"Ron, shut up!" May hissed so fiercely that Ron was quite taken aback. He gulped and shut his mouth.

"Snowflake," she said gently, "tell me how you feel,"

"I, I feel much better. T-Thank you for asking,"

"You are my half-sister, aren't you? Why should I not ask?" She asked, tickling her white bunny.

"Snowflake!" Tabitha mewed warmly.

"Tabitha!" the two hugged, in an animalish sort of way.

Just then, Ivy and Iris returned with a group of animals. There was a leopard, a zebra, a kingfisher, and a bear.

"These are for your parents," Iris said.

"They will choose whom they want," Ivy said. She ordered and the parents to stand in a line. After some time, the zebra went over to May's mother.

"Ruby chooses you as her special bond. To decline is a great outrage," Iris explained, after she saw the look of confusion on May's mother's face.

"I'll accept," She said, rather hastily, but smiling. She patted Ruby's head.

The bear, Thunder, went to Josh's father, the leopard, Jade, slunk over to Ron's mother. The kingfisher flew straight to Carra's father. They sat down with their kids with the animals sitting right behind them.

"Don't we have to be Ronens to bond?" Ron asked doubtfully. "Not necessary, Ron" Minkin said, turning his gaze to his little brown book.

"Who will go first?" Minkin asked. He looked at Carra with his sharp green eyes.

"I will," Carra said, clearly nervous and excited.

"Come front with whom you want to bond with," He instructed. Carra and Tabitha walked up to the fire, and stood there, unsure of what to do next. Minkin had his nose buried in his book. Finally he looked up and asked them to recite what he told them to.

"*We shall protect each other*" he said.

"*We shall protect each other,*" Carra and Tabitha said, one after another.

"*Until death,*"

"*Until death,*"

"*And never abandon each other,*"

"*And never abandon each other,*"

"I pledge that we will be together,"

"I pledge that we will be together,"

"And so shall rest as bonds," Minkin said.

"*And so shall rest as bonds,"* The two repeated together.

"Good. Now hold hands and bow down to Mother Earth," He instructed. They did as told and, just stood there. Nothing happened. They didn't feel any different. Minkin looked astonished. Another Ronen came running over and whispered something to Minkin. But Pal's sharp ears caught the words shared between the two Ronens.

"He said that we may be already bonded," Pal whispered. Everyone looked flabbergasted.

"Pal! You spoke without a mistake!" Ron cheered. "I did?" Pal looked astonished as well. "Yes!" Tabitha purred. Carra stared at her cat in wonder. Tabitha, who always growled and hissed at her arch-enemy, Pal, was actually purring at him now!

"I think that, since you were very close from a long time-" Minkin was interrupted by Ron. "From when I was seven"

"Since you were together for a long time, we think that you have already bonded naturally," Minkin finished, half glaring at Ron. "You will all have to say the oath, though," He added.

Five minutes later, they all finished the oath. But when each parent finished the oath, the ground shook once slightly, as if Mother Earth was acknowledging each bond and approving them. After May's mother, who was first, finished her oath, Avaron and some Ronens came dragging a monster behind them, whom they called The Dragon. May's heart began to beat faster and she felt all sorts of insects, mostly butterflies in her stomach. The monster was, in a way, *beautiful.* It had pretty purple and blue scales, and an attractive golden, blue and pink head. It was somewhat like a dragon, which was why it mostly got its name.

Avaron lead the Dragon to an isolated place, followed by May's mother and Ruby.

"Rise and shine, beauty!" Avaron shouted to the dragon, and it opened its eyes, revealing its magnificent greenish-blue eyes. Its eyes swivelled, taking in its surroundings, before finally resting on May's mother. It then stood up, yawned, revealing humongous teeth, and lunged towards Mrs. Sparks. May's mother screamed, which was echoed by May's.

10

Everyone was successfully bonded, and no one got eaten or burnt by the Dragon. They all came back happily; with Josh's father literally sitting on his bear. They both were laughing. May had run and hugged her mother the moment she came back. That was the test- the bonds had to save each other from the dragon, or 'whatever stupid beast it was' May thought.

Romial, a Ronen, also the commander of the army, and Avaron had tested the parents. Jade, Tabitha and Pal talked with each other while Pete and the kingfisher chased each other, playing fly-tag. Snowflake and the zebra, Ruby, who was quiet most of the time, became friends as well.

"Everyone! Gather!" a loud roar scared them out of their wits.

"Who's that?" Tabitha hissed, arching her back.

"I have never heard that before," Ruby said, confused.

"That is the mighty and valiant Chesternut," Victoria said laughing.

"Chesternut! What a joke!" Snowflake also laughed. Her friends joined her.

"Come, we had better go now," Iris managed to say, laughing at Pal's clumsy attempts to look like Chester.

They all moved to the base of a rock, where most of the clan had already gathered. They found some empty space near the front and stood there.

"We must leave now. It is getting late, and the trees are getting fewer and fewer. Are you and your bonds ready?" Avaron asked, standing on top of the rock.

"Yes!" they chorused. They moved here and there for last minute preparations. Ron just thought, what might it be like to be Pal? Would he be able to see colour once he is really bonded? Would his powers be transmitted to Pal and Pal's powers to him?

Ron was closing his eyes when he thought this. When he opened them, his vision was so accurate that he even noticed a little ant crawling on the ground so far away! He could smell everything! And his hearing, it was so accurate that he heard Josh and Iris talking about food. He looked at May next. She felt someone's eyes on her, and when she turned around, she screamed. Seeing her scream, Ron screamed, too, and he looked down. He was so short! And instead of hands, he had golden paws! He turned his head, and he could see his body was covered in fur and he had a tail! He screamed again. His voice came out hoarse, like a bark. He had become a dog!

Ivy came running to his aid. She asked him to calm down first. Then she told him to think about humans. After he did so, he had hands instead of paws, no tail, and he had become a boy again. Josh supported him, after seeing that he looked like he was going to faint and fall down. He took him to one of the caves nearby and he sat down, with his stomach churning and his head feeling giddy and dizzy. Finally, he fainted.

He came to after five minutes, and Iris told them that it was extra-ordinary that he transformed into an animal without formally even *becoming* a Ronen at all.

"Only real Ronens can transform into an animal without training. That too, is very rare. Transforming into animals is almost everything the teachers ever teach," She explained. Then she asked him how he managed to become a dog.

"I-I was just thinking about how Pal might see, I mean, if he saw everything in colour, or what and if after bonding, his p-powers would be shared with me and m- mine with him," He said shakily.

"It is fine. Do not worry. You will get used to it. You all just be with him. I will go tell Father," Ivy said. Ivy raced away towards the big cave. She came back and said it was most probably just the close bonding that they had, similar to being brothers and that they should all get ready soon. They were to leave in a few minutes.

They were soon all gathered with Chester and Avaron, the leaders at the front. They both walked out of the clearing with everyone behind them. Everyone had a basket of his or her own, which they would share with their bonds. Each basket contained two blankets, neatly folded, one retractable pillow, one cover in which there were fruits and vegetables, and other personal items which they need. The six kids walked alongside a boy who had a striking resemblance to the sisters. They found out that he was Leif, Ivy and Iris' brother. He was thin, but looked strong. He had auburn hair and green eyes, like his three sisters and his father. Ivy told them that he was one of their best hunters and fighters. Many people were in awe of him, because he hunted and fought so well.

That following night, they all slept nearby a river to quench their thirst, after eating some fruits. The six slept together, chattering until exhaustion pushed them to a deep sleep.

The following morning, Leif woke them up early. Carra, Ron and Josh groaned, especially Josh, who was a sleepy head. May was an early bird, and had no issue waking up so early. Ivy and Iris woke up at the same time every day, and so, had no problem.

Soon, they were all gathered around a huge fire. Josh was still yawning. Ron looked quite excited but sleepy. Carra was looking very dull. Only May was energetic.

"We have to move fast. It seems that some humans who had come to clear out the forest have noticed some kind of commotion in the forest yesterday, and have found our trail. They carry weapons and are probably getting closer and closer to our hideout as I speak," Avaron said calmly. Murmurs of horror and shock were heard. The humans weren't what the Ronens feared, it was the thought of the humans betraying their secret and the horrible thought of being sliced up by the human's weapons.

Avaron turned and left with Chester by his side. The rest followed him. They went at a quite fast pace. When they were out of the clearing, they heard a cry behind them. They turned around and saw a group of people rushing towards them. They started running, but the people also started running faster.

"What should we do?" Romial growled.

"Fight," Avaron answered calmly. The head of the Ronens positioned himself in the front with his faithful lion by him. The rest gathered in a formation behind their leaders. The humans rushed in first and the Ronens defended themselves bravely. Pete was nearly shot, but Josh and Skyer came to his aid. May was managing well, kicking and punching everyone who came near her. Snowflake was nearby, rushing to help her bond when necessary. Ivy and Victoria were fighting back to back, defending each other fiercely. Tabitha and Carra were trying to keep the path clear for each other. Ron and Pal, well, Ron was sitting on a huge Pal, bearing a sword, and just threatening the humans. He was not the kind of boy who liked bloodshed, he liked peace more. Iris was flying on the back of Ruben and killing everyone who was going near Lily.

Misty was keeping up a good job of saving Lily, too. Every Ronen was fighting for their bonds and their clan, not for themselves. Finally, the Ronens won. Not one human was spared. They did not want to kill the humans, but they had no choice.

***

"Where are we headed to?" Ruby asked for the last time.

"Back to our planet. Since four seasons ago, our clan has become stronger. We are more in number. Because of this, hopefully, victory and luck will be in our favour," Avaron answered finally. It was mid-day, and the climate was very hot. Snowflake finally sat down. She could not walk anymore. Since she was the size of a normal rabbit, May carried her. After a minute, Tabitha and Jade sat down too. Soon, everyone was sitting down. No one could make a step more without refreshments. They opened their baskets and drank water. Then they ate some fruits and talked for some time. How much ever he tried to coax them, Avaron could not convince the Ronens to budge an inch. In the end, he gave up and sat down.

"Chester, where was the portal? I do not remember clearly, but I do remember we had to go to a huge continent, and then to another one where we had to cross a wide river," Avaron asked. He was sitting away from the others so as their conversations should not be heard. But Ivy had become a little fly and was buzzing around, eavesdropping on her father. She came back and told her friends that the portal was located all the way in some huge, gigantic forest.

"It has to be the Amazon forest. It is the biggest forest. Mostly," May concluded. Josh agreed.

"He even mentioned a big continent, which was very barren and dry." Ivy added.

"That has to be Africa." Josh assumed. "But why do we have to go all around to Africa instead of just going through Mexico?" he asked.

"No idea," May shrugged. Nobody had a clue about what he was talking about.

"I think it is because there is something in that place which we have to take," Iris said thoughtfully.

"Then why not only a few of us go there and the rest directly go to South America?" Josh suggested.

"Good idea," Ron said. Iris, Carra and May agreed. Only Ivy was doubtful. "How do we tell Father about this?" she asked. No one had an answer.

11

"Father?" Ivy said nervously.

"Hello, Ivy. Sit down. So, you want only some of us to go to the desert and pick up the stones? That is fine with me. Will you and your friends do it?" Avaron said casually. Ivy was shocked. How did her father know all this? Then it hit her. He was their clan leader, after all. Someone would have been watching them, and he (or she) would have told Avaron. Simple.

"Y-yes," She said. "That is our idea. Yes," She said, regaining her composure.

"So, what stones do we have to collect?" Snowflake asked curiously, stepping out from behind a bush.

"I will tell you," He said. He stood up and stretched a bit, then he sat down again as the others came and sat in a circle around the chief.

"You will have to collect a ruby, a sapphire, a lapis lazuli, a topaz, an amethyst and a diamond. Only if we get all the gems can we open the portal that leads to our planet. Meet us in the forest within 3 weeks. Take four if you want. It is a long journey there, after all. I will give you directions. Chester, the map please," He said. The lion handed over a map to his bond, and Avaron unfolded the map, showing it to the kids and their bonds. Ron studied the map, and then jumped up.

"Well, what are we waiting for? Let's go!" he shouted enthusiastically.

"Wait. We need to pack our baskets and get ready for the journey. It is a long way to Africa. We can leave tomorrow. We will need a very good night's rest tonight," Pal said wisely. Everyone was surprised at his words. He was usually even sillier, clumsier and stupider than Ron. And now, suddenly, he was so smart! They looked at him, amazed and baffled.

"We will travel a little closer to the Place of the Gems today, for your benefit. Then, we shall separate, and the rest of us will go directly to the other forest. Is that fine with all of you?"

"Of course, Father. That is very much fine with us,"

"Very well then. Tell the clan about these changes," Avaron commanded. His lion nodded abruptly and shot off.

"How will we go to Africa? We have to cross the whole Atlantic Ocean to get there! And when we do reach there, Africa is the second biggest continent. Where do we search? Are the gems scattered everywhere around? Or-" Josh was cut off mid-sentence.

"Wait patience!" Avaron chuckled. "I will arrange something. I will tell Minkin; he is also a magician, to do something. You all need not worry,"

"Then why not just ask Minkin to just, you know, make the gems appear?" Ron asked, in a way to not offend Avaron.

"That actually requires much more skills than Minkin has, because all those gems possess some magic themselves, which is almost the same amount of Minkin's. To do anything with them magically, other than tracing them on the map, one would need double the amount of magic the gems have," Avaron explained.

"What about the ocean? There are sharks there! And whales!" Ron gulped. "And jellyfish! And octopuses! And who knows what!" he cried.

Avaron looked annoyed. He wondered how such a freaked out kid could cope up on such a perilous journey, 'but his friends are there' he thought.

"Ron's scared because whales are the largest animals in the world. Ron, calm down. Whales are very, very extra gentle creatures. And not all jellyfish are poisonous. Nor are octopuses. And only 35 species of shark are dangerous," May said, trying to console her scaredy-pants friend. She knew all about animals. "And anyways, Ron, I do not believe anyone told anything about swimming in the ocean," Avaron said.

"We're not swimming?" Ron asked.

"No, you are not. We had better start off then. We have a long way to go today," Avaron said and stood up. He waved to the kids to follow and walked back to where the rest of the Ronens were gathered.

"Come. We should leave today. I presume Chester has told you of our plans?" he asked.

"Yes. But still, how can you send these children on their own?" Romial asked, sceptical.

"They are not alone. I am going with them," a bold voice came. They turned around and saw Leif striding towards them. "So am I," Leif's bond, Topaz said.

"No, son. I need you here. Ruben and Victoria shall take care of them. They are brave and strong on their own. Ivy also has nearly completed her training. They will manage fine by themselves," Avaron said firmly.

"Come, Father. We are ready to go," Iris said. The leader signalled for his clan to follow him.

They walked on for three hours, stopping here and there from time to time. The hunters gathered fruit as they moved.

Soon, as the day came to an end, the moon smiled brightly and everyone sat down to rest. Only the six friends bustled around, collecting stuff and packing it into their baskets.

"Kids, you should sleep now. You have a long day ahead of you, and it won't do you any good if you don't sleep well tonight,"

May sighed. It was just like her mother to say that, but she knew her mother was right. She turned around. Even Ron's mother and Josh's father were standing behind hers.

"Get up, Ron. You have to go sleep. I'll pack your basket," Ron's mother said. Ron yawned and got up lazily, but he was kind of shocked. His mother usually scolded and shouted at him to get him out of bed and do his work before sleeping, and now, here he was, being told by his mother to go and sleep! But he knew that, since he had a long day, accompanied by a longer journey, ahead of him, he needed to sleep early. He was trying to stuff a load of food, and had failed a number of times, so he just left it to his mother and walked away, while his mother pulled back the sleeves of her t-shirt and got down to work.

The six went to a grassy patch, snuggled up and slept. Ron started to snore almost immediately. May's mother smiled as she packed her daughter and Carra's baskets.

"Well, even if we are going to see them in a month, it seems like they are going away for........ forever," Ron's mother said ruefully.

"Yes, but... What can we do? It seems to be fate," Mrs Sparks said. She was a little superstitious, and believed in fate and destiny. She sighed as she gazed at her daughter, sleeping so comfortably, snuggled up with Snowflake. She turned her head away and saw that May's water bottle was left out. She pushed it into the basket, and then got up. She walked away, her legs a little stiff, and was followed by Carra's father.

Ron's mother, finally managing to stuff two extra sandwiches and one extra cake, closed the lid of the basket tightly, but no matter how hard she tried, she couldn't get it closed. Carra's father also came to help, but to no avail. Finally, Josh's father suggested they put some of their son's food into Josh's basket. Anyhow, Josh never ate much, so his basket was light. They tried that and succeeded. They walked away, satisfied and went to sleep themselves.

12

"Are we there yet?" Ron asked for the millionth time. The six and their bonds had aimed for North America's border, New York. Minkin had made the whole way to New York look like a forest. However, the humans outside the clan could not see the change and life continued normal outside the spell. They had been travelling for four days now. The forest made it much easier to travel since they could just walk through mountains and walk over lakes as if they weren't even there. They had been walking from morning, and it was around noon now.

"I am sitting down," Ron said defiantly and flopped onto the ground, exhausted and annoyed that everyone else (except for Pal that is) ignored him and refused to stop to at least, let him *sit* down.

They turned back, exasperated with him. But seeing him sitting down and resting while they were tired and standing was too much for them. They slumped down and were relieved that the grass was cool, though the weather was searing hot. Tabitha rolled over, scratching her back. She stayed like that for some time, expecting a belly rub, and she got one from May, who was too tempted to do it. Tabitha let out a purr of satisfaction and happiness.

"Lucky you. You at least can get something you like around here," May said, giggling. They continued on their journey, but not before eating a bit and snoozing for some time.

When the day came to an end, they had managed to reach the borders of New York. They ate and drank, then decided to sleep. They took out their blankets and pillows, and while they lay down, they chatted and talked till their dreams pushed them into a deep sleep. They took turns guarding, and decided that two should guard while the rest sleep. Every two hours, they would swap their positions. Ruben and Iris offered the first shift, and Josh was more than glad that he was not chosen for the first shift. He could get quite grumpy if he does not have enough sleep!

Carra and Tabitha were on duty when the rays of the rising sun broke into the still, cold air, warming up the earth with his radiant smile. The two decided to wake up the rest, as they thought that it would be best if they make an early start. May was a light sleeper, and she woke up to the sound of leaves crunching under Tabitha's paws. She stretched, and helped her friends to rouse the others. Snowflake was just like her bond, and woke easily, and so did Ivy, her sister and their bonds. Even Ron and Pal were not that tough to wake up. The only problem was Josh and Pete. They tried everything they could- they shouted, they pushed him; they even kicked and punched him! But still, Josh did not wake up.

In the end, they had to drag him all the way. And only when his hand hit a rock did he wake up!

Everyone heaved a sigh of relief and continued, giving Josh the tiniest of tiny breaks to freshen up.

"Wait up!" he cried, racing to catch up with his friends. Thankfully, he was as fast in running as he was in falling asleep. He caught up with the others, panting and huffing. He bent over to catch his breath. He ran a hand through his blonde hair as he walked slowly, clutching his side. Ron walked slowly so that he would be in pace with his friend, and helped Josh.

Josh was walking so slowly that Ron couldn't concentrate on anything but the ground. Finally, when Josh said "Let's go," Ron looked up, but saw no one there! Then, as he squinted and scrunched up his eyes, he saw some specks in the far off distance. He gave a yelp and ran to catch up with his friends. Josh also ran, but easily over took Ron. They finally reached their friends, who had not even noticed the disappearance of the two boys, save for Pete and Pal.

They walked on and on and on until they finally reached the water side of New York. They stared, dumbfounded and gaped at the strange sight in front of them. The forest even crossed the ocean!

Ivy, not one to waste time, was already a bit way down when the others came out of their astonishment. Victoria nudged Snowflake, and the two made their way into the forest. The rest followed. They could still see the ocean though, through the forest because the forest floor was made of leaves, which left some space for them to see the raging waves beneath them. At nightfall, they realized that the forest here was kind of narrow, which did not leave them enough space to sleep side by side. So they decided to scatter and sleep. This time, Iris and May offered for the shift at the same time, so they both watched over their friends.

"Do you have any idea how to find the gems?" May asked.

"They must be on the map," Iris answered, and pulled out the map from her sister's basket.

"So... Hmm. It seems that the Ruby is right on the... Right here," She pointed at a small, flickering, red spot on the outskirts of the continent. She looked at May, expecting her to tell her where that spot was. May recognised the look.

"Oh no. I'm sorry. I'm not good in geography. If you want something on animals, I'm there. But something like this, Josh is the answer," May apologized.

"I will ask him tomorrow then," Iris said and settled down to gaze at the stars.

"Is that a hobby of yours?" May asked.

"What?"

"Stargazing,"

"Yes. I usually cloud gaze, sky gaze and star gaze as well!" Iris giggled. May snorted. "And maybe you can add planet-gazing too, because some people say that some stars up there are actually planets. Who knows, right?" Iris said, squinting up at the stars.

"Yep, but scientists do, and they never seem to spread information correctly," May said. Iris giggled.

They spent the rest of their time together talking about constellations and galaxies. Iris even learnt about nebulas.

13

"What?" Josh moaned.

Iris and May had fretted over on how to wake up Josh. He was assigned for the next shift, and thankfully, managed to wake up Josh at the second attempt. He and Pete took over the duty, but retired after one hour only, and woke up Carra and Ivy, who wanted to take a turn together.

After the next two days as a trial, Ruben finally found a way to wake up Josh. Just lift him into the air and fly away. And that's exactly what they did. Pete and Ruben each took one hand and flew away, and soon, the others could hear shouts and cries for help. But it ceased soon. Josh was not that easily frightened, but still, it would be pretty scary if a person woke up to be suspended above a huge ocean with two birds carrying him away.

The birds came back, carrying a calm Josh, who looked very embarrassed.

They continued, and, after one week of the same landscape, they reached Africa's border. They immediately unrolled the map, and found that the ruby was lying rather close. The forest ended there, but, there weren't many people living in Africa, because of the spell, they had been moved to other continents for a short time. The magician had told them that there will be six silver dots, representing Ivy, Iris, May, Carra, Ron and Josh, and six white dots standing for their bonds. Now, when they checked the map, they saw that they were on the map, with their names beside the respective spot. They decided to split up into groups of 4. Ivy stood up as the leader, and no one stopped her. She was the eldest, after all.

"Ron, Josh, Pal and Pete, you will form team A. Iris, you, Carra and your bonds will be team B. Victoria, Snowflake, May and I will be team C. Team A, you will move north. Team B, you move west, and we will move east. Everyone should please make a note of which gems will come your way," Ivy said.

"There is no need for that, sister. Father has given us two extra maps. They are not that accurate, but they will do," Iris said, pulling out two maps from her basket. She passed one to Ron, and kept the other with herself. She let her sister keep the original one. Then they parted, after what seemed to Josh a pointless waste of fifteen minutes of embracing each other for farewell.

They had four walkie-talkies, and the three teams took one each, the leaving the last one to be a spare.

They journeyed on, sending reports of their situations, finds and dangers they faced to the others.

The first team to find a gem was team B.

"Hey, we found a gem! We got the topaz. It was hidden pretty well. When we reached the spot, it was in a village! We had to search the entire place, which included ransacking a few big and wealthy houses, but that was just to restock our food. I think the gems are all in villages or towns. It was rather tough, but we found it in some guy's hat, which looked more like a crown," Tabitha reported.

"How does it look like?" Ron asked excitedly.

"It gleams, and is more golden and bright than the very sun," Iris said softly into the walkie-talkie. She was awe-struck.

Sighs came from the other end, as the others tried to imagine how the gems might be.

***

"Hello?" Victoria's voice crackled in the walkie-talkie.

"We're here," Josh replied.

"We can't find the ruby," May said.

"What!"

"Why not?"

"Hold on, guys! The ruby just keeps jittering here and there! It's just jumping from house to house! How do we catch it?" May asked.

"I think it is best if you leave the ruby for now. Find the other gems, and then we'll all come and help you to search for the ruby after we find the rest of the gems," Iris suggested.

"That's a good plan," Ron approved.

There was a background barking, and everyone knew that Pal clearly agreed with his bond.

They started to get the other gems, and not before long, Josh's triumphant voice was heard through their devices, claiming that his team had found the lapis lazuli.

"All right!" May cheered.

"Back to work," Ivy said, and they resumed their hunt. Not before long-

"The diamond!" Ruben's excited voice was heard.

"You've got it!"

"Cool,"

"How does it look like?"

"It glitters. It shines. It's a crystal. How was the lapis lazuli? You never told us," Iris accused Ron and Josh.

"It's blue, shining and amazing," Josh said.

"So, this is the village, is it?" Carra asked. May nodded. The other teams, after having found the rest of the gems, had come to help May and her team find the ruby. "The ruby never left the village; we kept checking. It just jumps from house to house. What the heck should we do?" Snowflake asked. They all thought.

"I got an idea!" May cried suddenly. Carra smiled warmly. She knew it wouldn't be long before her friend would hit upon a genius brainwave.

"The map shows the location of the stones, doesn't it? We could all visit one house each, and wait for the ruby to appear. It can't skip the houses, can it? At one point or the other, it will have to come into at least one of our houses. We can catch it then," May suggested.

"That is true, but we might miss it, if we are in a big house. I say, we can first just see if the ruby follows a pattern, like if it goes into this house, it will go into that one every time. Then we can easily determine which house it will strike next, right? If it doesn't follow a pattern, then we can go ahead with May's plan," Ivy said. "Yes, that is a good plan. They all studied their respective maps for a while. After the ruby completed two rounds around the whole village, Victoria caught onto the pattern. "I got it! It goes like this," She traced the pattern with her paw. "Good thinking, Vic," Ivy said, and they immediately went into the next-to-next house and spread around. When the ruby attacked, they felt a slight tremor passing through, and a high-pitched squeal, like somebody was trapped and wanted to be free, was heard. Pete squawked too, like he was wrestling with something. The sound of flapping wings was heard, and everyone rushed to the room where Pete was. He was trying to hold a very squirming ruby in his claws. Ruben immediately relieved Pete of the ruby. The ruby was no match for Ruben's strong grip. "Congratulations, Pete! You have got the ruby!" Ivy smiled. Everyone cheered loudly, and decided to leave at once. Ruben put the wiggling ruby into the bag which held the other gems, and it at once quietened down. They all had been gone for nearly three weeks now, and they didn't want to be too late. They immediately set off out of the house.

They were, anyways, luckily in the edge of Africa, next to the Atlantic Ocean, so they quickly searched for the forest bridge, and when Ruben found it, they headed there and raced across in an attempt to cross it as fast as possible. They ran so hard that they crossed almost half the bridge in one day. They made it in the next one and a half days, and instantly rushed across but were so tired that they nearly collapsed a quarter through New York. They did not even stop to see the wonderful skyscrapers or the Statue of Liberty. It did not occur to them that that day would be the only chance for them to see the monument, for they were going back to the Ronen planet.

When they finally reached the border, they found that there was a blue portal, leaning against a huge tree, one which was not easy to miss. They were first captivated, which changed into intimidation, then suspicion, until finally, they sent Ruben to look inside when curiosity got the better of them. But, even after sometime, they did not get a response. Iris became frantic and nearly fainted. Suddenly-

"Iris! Everyone! Do not worry! I have found Avaron! This portal leads to our clan!" his reassuring voice was heard through the portal. All of them heaved a big sigh of relief, and jumped in, one by one.

14

"Mom!" a cry rang out through the gurgle of the fierce river flowing beside them. They were in the Amazon jungle.

"May?" her mother turned around. "May! You're back!" they ran to each other, and May was nearly choked in the process of getting hugged by her mother.

"Dad!" Josh shouted as he dashed to his father. Ron was on the verge of tears on seeing his mother.

Carra beamed with joy as she explained how their quest went on to her father.

"Iris! Ivy!" Lily squealed. She raced to her sisters with Leif on her heels. Avaron followed, unable to hide his relief and happiness on seeing his daughters safe and sound. The animals too, were happy to be reunited with their friends.

After hugging his daughters, he smiled warmly and asked, "May I please see the stones?"

Ivy grinned and shook her head. "Oh no?" her father said. He raised an eyebrow in amusement, but was still smiling.

He reached out to grab her, but she jumped out of the way. She quickly passed the gems to her sister, but Iris was not fast enough. Her father caught her. She laughed and begged Avaron to let her go. Then she opened the purse and took out the gems, one by one, and showed it to the Ronens gathered around her.

"Father, when we tried to catch the ruby, it kept jumping here and there. Why?" Iris asked.

"I had told you, remember, that the gems possess some quantity of magic themselves? Well, this ruby has more magic than the rest. That is why it keeps hopping about," Avaron explained.

"What are they used for, by the way?" Lily asked curiously.

"Wait and watch, Lily," Leif said, patting her shoulder.

Avaron took the little purse and walked towards a tall tree. He paused, and then took out a stone, which happened to be the Lapis lazuli. He felt for something in the tree, and apparently found it. He then proceeded to place the night-blue gem into a small carving on the tree trunk. He did the same for the rest. Everyone fell silent as he finished putting the last stone, the diamond in place. He stepped back, closed his eyes and chanted something, the Ronens were imitating him.

"What do we do?" Carra hissed to Iris.

"Just do not do anything. The children need not say this oath. This requires only the adults," Iris whispered back.

"A few years later, even I will have to say oaths and pledges and all those things," Ivy made a face. Ron laughed.

"When does this get over?" Josh asked. He was getting restless, and so was May. The animals were all in a corner of the group, and they were all talking softly to each other.

"Shh!" Leif hissed. "We are not supposed to talk during this oath!" the tall boy murmured, and turned back to chanting. Iris stuck her tongue out at her elder brother. Seeing her sister, it took all of Ivy's strength to not burst out laughing.

But she stopped grinning when thunder broke out through the sky.

"What is happening?" Lily wailed.

"Hush! It is ok," Leif comforted her.

"What *is* happening?" Iris asked.

"It is just the portal opening. Do not worry. Nothing will happen to us. We are safe here," Leif answered.

Soon enough, the ground in front of the leader broke. The leader addressed his clan.

"Ronens, the time has come that we return to our homeland. We must be strong, brave and courageous. Do not expect too much. They might have done anything to our home. They might have even destroyed our entire land and built a new empire. If so, we must fight bravely, and later, spend a lot of time and work hard towards rebuilding our home town,"

Ron looked down the deep hole. "Whoa. That's pretty deep!" he said nervously.

"We have to jump in," Carra poked her finger into her cousin's back. "How do you know?!" Ron asked, panicked.

"Duh. That's the portal. Go figure," She rolled her eyes. Ron gulped. Pal looked like he was about to burst out laughing.

"Romial and I will go first. You will all follow," Avaron said. His three elder children nodded. "Come. We shall go," Avaron said. With that, Ronen and bond jumped into the hole/portal together. Romial and his bond followed, and then the rest of the clan jumped in, bond by bond.

"I'm not going!" Ron wailed.

"Ron. Get. In," His mother warned. Ron didn't budge, but Pal did the job for him. He pushed Ron off the edge, and then jumped in himself. They heard Ron's scream for far too long than they expected to.

His mother shrugged and jumped in with her bond. May just lifted her eyebrow at Carra, then jumped in, followed by Josh, Carra and their animals.

Iris sat on Ruben's back, and they flew down together, and right behind them were Ivy and Victoria. As they fell, they noticed that, from rocky and hard, the walls had changed to grassy, smooth and soft. After some time, they realized that they weren't exactly falling; they were more sort of *gliding* down the portal. It was a long way down, but they were sure that they would end up in their home planet.

Suddenly, a deafening scream echoed out, and then, an ear-splitting, hoarse bark followed. Everyone knew at once that it was Ron who had screamed. They turned around and saw him with his hand over his mouth, pointing at the tunnel wall. Pal was repeatedly barking, and it was echoing all around. The Ronens looked around and saw creepy insects which had a scorpion's tail, eight spider legs, and a drooling cockroach head, on the walls, scurrying down to the Ronens, gnashing their teeth with hunger. But before they could react or even make a sound at the spooky insects, a blinding flash spread through the tunnel and no one remembered what happened next.

15

"Where are we?" Josh moaned.

"Ow! Ow! Get off, fatso! You're squishing me!" Carra cried.

"I am not fat!" Pal whimpered obstinately.

"At least get off!" Snowflake squeaked angrily.

"Tell Ron to!"

"Move over, Josh! My hand's going to be like a pancake then!" May cried.

Ivy finally came over and helped them up, freeing May's hand and pushing Josh and Ron off Pal and May. Then, pushing Pal off, she freed Pete, Snowflake and Carra. Tabitha helped Carra and Snowflake.

"Finally! Took you long enough," Ron complained.

"Be thankful! I need not have even helped you!" Ivy scowled. Pal just shook his shaggy coat and fur flew everywhere.

"Where are we?"Josh repeated his question.

"This place... It's awfully amazing!" Carra breathed. That was true. Here, the trees had green trunks and pink leaves. The sky had violet cloud-like structures streaked with purple, and the sky itself was fully light green. Curious little blue and orange animals which had a long neck on broad shoulders hopped about on six, plump legs in front of the newcomers.

Romial gasped. "It is the Bluteers! After all those years! I thought that they would have changed by now!"

"So did I," Avaron agreed.

The so-called Bluteers squeaked happily on seeing the Ronens.

They decided to stop a bit to rest. "Imagneus... it has been a very long time," Ivy murmured.

"Is Imagneus the name of this place?" May asked.

"Yes," Iris said, and they both continued to tell the story of their planet.

"It all started on a peaceful day. There were no trimles, or clouds, as you call them. No rain either. But as night fell, it started pouring, lightning flashed, thunder rumbled, and pretty soon, it started hailing as well. Everyone was surprised. We all gathered in our caves. Then we saw Grinlaut," Ivy clenched her fists. Iris continued-

"Grinlaut is a Streo, but an evil one. Streos are tall Imagneus creatures, but you cannot actually give a description of them. They all differ from one another. Some even look like worms, some look like bizarre creatures. Nothing was wrong in Grinlaut's family, the evil started in him. He was jealous-jealous of happiness and beauty, because he had caught a rare disease which made him always sad and ugly. It was curable, by beauty, a sort of beauty which chose him. He did not understand that, and instead, forced beauty to join him. But of course, that will not cure him. So, he decided to face the fact that he was ugly, but it was tough, of course. So, he became angry and revenge for his punishment filled him. You see, our mother's grandfather had put this curse on Grinlaut, for killing his bond on purpose. So, for revenge, he came with his army, all Hikints, and started devastating the place. We"Iris gestured at her sister and herself "and Lily were too young to fight, but Leif fought, and killed at least fifty Hikints that very day. He is a marvellous fighter. But they were too strong, and we had to retreat. They drove us out of our very own home," Iris's voice cracked. Ivy took it up from there-

"Father knew of a way out-a portal. But, he did not know where it led to. So he sent Chester through the portal to make sure it was safe, and then let the rest go. But he did not know that Grinlaut had taken some Ronens prisoner. Father thought that everyone had passed through and later when he did a check on everyone he..," Ivy broke off.

"He found that Mother was missing. She had been taken by Grinlaut too," Iris said, on the verge of tears.

"That is so sad!" May cried.

"Yes! I mean, if your mother was dead, that is one thing. But knowing that your mother is alive but not able to see her is horrible!" Josh exclaimed.

"How can you live without a mother?" Ron sniffled. He was about to cry. Everyone imagined their lives without a mother. It was utterly terrible!

"Any way, now that we are here again, I suppose we do have a chance of meeting her again," Iris said.

"Poor Lily. She does not even know how Mother looked like," Ivy said softly.

"Oh my goodness. That is even sadder!" Carra said.

"How did she look like?" Tabitha asked.

"She was tall, fair, and had black hair, which was very straight. You see Raptor there?" Ivy pointed to a big, black lion (animals here could be of any colour. There was the story of a light green puma which had saved its bond from an eagle since the eagle could not see the puma in the sky!) "He is our mother's bond,"

"Both your parents have lions as bonds!" Josh said.

"Leaders always have lions or tigers as bonds. Whatever animal is the leader's bond will always change into a lion or tiger, and his memory will be erased, leading him to believe that he had been a lion or tiger since birth," Iris explained.

"Wow! That's cool,"

"How does that happen?" May wanted to know. As usual, she was always interested in biology.

"Do not look at me. I have failed in biology. No interest," Ivy laughed. "You failed too?" Ron asked, surprised and happy. "Wow. Someone to join your group," Carra teased.

"Some diffusion of cells and molecules and blah blah blah," Iris said.

"Not blah blah blah, it is the changing of cellular structure, DNA, skeletal structure, and atoms," Someone said. Everyone jumped around, shocked. It was Leif. He had sneaked up behind them.

"When a Ronen becomes leader, his own cells change. During the ceremony, he has to hold hands and pledge or whatever with his bond. Then, when they touch, the cells get transferred to his bond and his bond changes as well,"

"If you need anything, ask Leif the almighty," Iris joked, rolling her eyes mockingly.

"Oh really? I will show you to ask an almighty person," Leif said and shot off after his sister, who crashed into Lily and Avaron. Leif too smashed into them at full speed, and as he fell down, pulled Ivy down as well, as she was standing nearby.

"The royal fall!" Snowflake laughed.

"Nice one, Snow!" May giggled.

"Presenting, the Royale Fall movie," Ron said in a funny, voice, bowing down and waving his arms around. Josh and Pal cracked up totally at this, and soon, they too were tangled up on the ground.

"Oh, well. Presenting, the Common Fall movie, then," He said in the same voice.

"Stop that, Ron," Josh groaned. "And Pal, get off! Man, you're heavy!"

"Hey, I'm only 39 kilos!" Pal protested.

"And you think I'm strong enough to bear that weight!" Josh complained.

"You should be! I'm not that heavy."

"Stop it, you two! You guys always disturb my grooming," Tabitha rolled her eyes.

"Whatever."

Carra helped Ivy up, while May helped Iris to stand.

"You okay?" May asked.

"Yeah. Yes. Sort of. Yep, I'm fine," Iris said, massaging her head.

"Iris, you should *see* where you run. You too, Leif," Avaron helped his youngest daughter to stand.

"Iris, I am still holding a grudge at you. Only this time, it is more," Leif said, and again, they raced around the Ronens. Josh too, joined, and soon, everyone was chasing each other. Leif's bond, a python named Topaz, finally somehow, managed to catch Josh, which was really a great achievement.

They played tag for a long time, to keep their mind of the dangerous situation, until they collapsed out of exhaustion. They rested for some time, but they had to cover a lot of ground before night fall. They moved along unknown lands, which was once so familiar to them.

They travelled deep into the night, and set off as soon as the silvery-gray sun rose. Finally, when Avaron actually told 'we are here' instead of 'we are almost there', three days had passed.

The friends looked around in bewilderment. They had run off to find the Ronen's former hometown, and had expected to find a pink (since the plants here was pink, it has to be pink, and not green like on Earth.) lush, blooming place where the trapped Ronens were running around freely, but what met their eyes was worse than Hell itself. Little eerie insects which scuttled like spiders were swarming around jagged rocks which grew from nowhere at all, and burnt, gray trees stood like guards around a creepy, giant rock in the middle of the clearing. As they watched, a humongous figure emerged from the rock-cave. He turned his face in the children's direction, and they gasped as his gaze ran over them. He was even worse than every ugly creature combined together! He had an awful, red, burnt face with evil, red eyes, the colour of rich blood. He had thorns sticking out of every bare patch of skin on his forehead, and a bunch of slimy, green snakes with red eyes formed his hair. His teeth were black and so sharp that just a tiny hole from it would last forever. A green tongue, forked like a snake's, kept flickering in and out of his mouth. His back was covered with spikes as well, and he had four horns on his face-two on his head, like a cow's, and two emerging from his cheeks. His nose, well, it was just two holes on his face. Ron almost fainted dead right away. Even Josh started perspiring out of fear.

"That, that awful c-creature is Grinlaut!" Ivy hissed.

"I'm so angry I could go and kill him in my bare hands. Right now!" Iris's voice cracked as she spoke. "Calm down, Iris!" May whispered. "You'll have your revenge. Soon, but not now,"

"I know, but still," Iris turned away and managed to smile. "Come, Father would be planning the battle. We had better not miss it," She said to the others. They disappeared from behind the bush.

When they reached the place where they had pitched their camp, Avaron had already started the battle plan. But they did not miss out much, and whatever they did, Leif filled in later.

"Everyone should get good night's sleep. Tomorrow is a big day for all of us. We will attack at dusk," Avaron addressed his clan mates. He went over to his lion, and sat down beside him.

"Do not worry, Avaron. We will defeat them. You should rest now. Leave your troubles behind you," Carra heard Chester tell his bond.

"Wake up! Rise and shine! The sun's up already!" May tried to wake her friends up. Finally, Carra and Ron woke up, but of course, Josh didn't. Ron became impatient and kicked his friend's leg. Josh jumped up with shock.

"What's your hurry?" He grumbled as he pushed his blanket off him.

"Don't you know?" Carra asked, rolling her eyes.

"Oh! The battle!" Josh smacked his head. He jumped out and raced to the lake nearby to brush and wash his face.

The other three were waiting for him by a big tree. Leif joined them and informed them about some minor changes in the plans. As they looked around, they saw that everyone were busy. Everyone were hustling and bustling here and there, doing this and that. The four joined the crowd packing up their weapons. But of course, Ron didn't. But after some persuading, Ron finally agreed to pose as a distraction as long as it didn't involve fighting. "But you will need something. A sword or a knife. Just in case," Avaron said, handing over a collection of weapons. Ron chose a dagger and looked like he killed someone just by holding the knife.

Josh started waving around, doing battle moves with a silver and green hilt sword, but that only made Pete laugh a lot. May took a bow and some arrows, and moved away to practice on something, and Carra followed with a couple of daggers.

The animals decided to practice with what they had Beaks, claws, teeth and talons. They spent the day in getting as much training as possible. May learnt to shoot bull's eye in just half an hour. Even Ron could throw a dagger into the bull's eye without his hand shaking too much.

"I hope that everyone is ready for the battle, for there is no time left. You must all fight hard, and everyone should try their very best. If we lose, well..," He could not continue his sentence. "Come then, we should not waste any more time,"

Chester immediately bounded up to his side, and they walked out with the Ronens following them. They went slowly, for they did not know what to expect, and each was imagining their home in different ways. But what met their eyes was worse than how it looked in even the most imaginative mind. Only the six friends had seen it earlier, when the saw Grinlaut, and were not that shocked. In their haste to practice and get prepared for the battle ahead, none of the six could tell anyone else of the state of the Ronen's home.

From the giant rock in the middle, screams could be heard.

"No! Let go! Ok fine! I'll do it! Just leave my daughter alone," A shrill female voice shrieked.

"Not enough. I'll leave your daughter, but your son is coming with me. I need this done, or your sister goes. After your son," A gruff voice said which most certainly was Grinlaut.

"No!" the female voice screamed again. "I'll do it! I'll do everything. Just leave my family alone," "Go check it, will you Ivy? Take Iris and your friends," Avaron begged. He was very concerned about the person who screamed.

"Yes Father," Ivy said. She was already creeping towards the rock, hidden by some bushes. Her friends and Iris were right behind her. But close to the entrance were four soldiers, and to pass them unnoticed was impossible. When they were creeping back, Josh noticed something. "Look! A back entrance!" Josh pointed out.

"Good! We shall go. Single file, everyone. Iris at front. I will go last. No one should make a sound. Go, Iris," She hissed, and her sister immediately started crawling forward. Iris managed to get inside without being seen. Ruben instantly followed her, shrinking as he flew. Tabitha sprang forward, looking around before disappearing into the rock. Carra darted safely into the rock as well. But Ron messed it. He went like a detective alright- rolling on the ground, looking around before hurrying up, but just as he was going into the crevice, a hefty soldier, who looked kind of like an elephant with a crocodile's head, turned around and spied the boy.

"*Aarughh! Gagd hakdh lokhzsha!*" He roared. None of them could make out heads or tails from what he said. They, however, understood three things- he had seen Ron, he was very angry and he was coming to get them!

Thankfully, no one else had heard the croc-elephant screaming, so when May stuck out her foot and tripped the soldier, no one came to his aid. Josh immediately bopped the crocodile head, and he went out cold. Ivy heaved a sigh of relief, and Pal scuttled across the mud path to get to the rock. no one disturbed their line after that, and everyone made it across safely. They peered in, and spotted Grinlaut standing over a thin woman who seemed very scared. She was, apparently, the one who had screamed out. And indeed, there was a young girl by her side and a small boy in Grinlaut's arms.

"How do we rescue them?" Pal asked Ivy.

"You will not," A husky voice said behind them. A pair of meaty hands grabbed Josh and Ron by their shirt necks and threw them to another soldier standing nearby. The four girls stood and stared at the bulk of a man standing behind them as he grabbed a rope and faster than lightning, tied Ruben and Pete's beaks and talons and threw them to the soldier as well. The croc-elephant came in, raving like a mad man. He stopped when he saw the friends, two already tied up. He tied up the girls, grinning while the Hulk man locked them up.

"What do we do?" Snowflake wailed.

"It's okay. Calm down," May soothed.

"How?" cried Ron. "We're trapped in here with a bunch of fatsos guarding us and the clan is relying on us to help them you expect us to be calm?" he blubbed.

"Shut up, Ron! They might hear you!" Carra hissed.

But, apparently, it seemed that neither of the guards had heard Ron. They looked around in dismay. Grinlaut had seen their capture. He came close, and licked his mouth, which was dribbling with his green saliva.

"What a welcome," He said, grasping the bars of the cage. "You will be all a delicious food for me," He slurped. "You first learn how to speak English. Then we'll see about food," Josh retorted. Grinlaut banged the cage bars in fury, but Josh just stood there, not wavering. Finally, Grinlaut went away, but the friends did not see where he went. They all started cooking up plans. Finally, Ivy remembered something. "These guys, they cannot swim, nor run very fast," She said slowly, thinking.

"I think I have got an idea!" she exclaimed suddenly. "No, it will not work," She said the next moment.

"It might, Ivy. Tell us," May said.

"We can maybe change it a bit to work if it is very good," Iris suggested.

"Well, I thought maybe we could, you know..,"

16

"Hey. Hey! You! Yeah, you! Fatso! I'm hungry. Get me some food. A burger," Josh said, yawning to the Hulk man.

"Erggh?" He grunted. "Bugger? You want bug? Here, take bug," He showed a bitten cockroach kind of insect, which he was eating.

"Yuck! No, not a bug, a burger! Just get me some food. What sort of food do you have here?" he asked.

"You want Pitsaa? Pitsaa good. Hmm," He snorted, gulped the rest of the insect, and called out to the croc-elephant. "Hidjerst! Kiths aneufjig pitsaa!" he shouted.

"He knows what a pizza is?" Josh asked, disbelievingly to Iris.

"No, he asked for a pitsaa. Do not worry. It is quite a delicious dish eaten here. I love it!" She assured him.

"That's a pitsaa?" Carra asked, pointing at the stuff piled up on a plate in Crocphant's hand-hoofs.

"Huh?" Ivy was busy trying to make fire by rubbing two

stones. She looked up. "Oh, yeah. That is a pitsaa," She stood up, and kicked the stones back. "They also have bad eyesight," She whispered as he came nearer with the food. They had all removed the ropes that had bound them, by using the dagger which Ron had pocketed. Strangely, the guards noticed, but were either too dumb to realize that they could cause harm if they were free, or they were too sleepy or lazy to bother retying them.

He bent and pushed the pitsaa in between the bars of their cage. "Enjooy," He said hoarsely, and walked away to a little cot to doze off.

Iris pulled the food towards her sister. She acted like she was about to eat when it caught fire!

"What the-" she cried, standing up instantly. Ivy winked at her sister.

"Help! Help!" Ruben cried. The Hulk man immediately came running.

"Wot happen?" He asked.

"Fire! Can't you see?" Iris cried.

"Get some water, nut head!" May yelled.

The Hulk-man ran away, (though it was surprising that he could even jog, considering his bulk!) and rushed back with a bucket of water. He threw open the gate and raced in, about to throw the water. But Josh was quicker. Ivy had also told them that if water splashes into their eyes, they will not be able to see for a whole day. Only the next day will they recover. So, Josh instantly punched the bucket of water, (but Pete did most of the work, by holding the rim of the bucket with his talons to tilt it the other way around.) and the bucket toppled over on Hulk-man's face, blinding him. The kids and their bonds let out a happy cry and raced outside, once again tripping over Crocphant and leaving him knocked out. The other guards had all gone for their lunch.

"Yes!" Ron whooped once they got out.

"Do not celebrate yet. We still have some unfinished work to do inside," Iris reminded him.

"If you do, then go do it. Just don't drag me in, okay?" Ron said, exasperated. He was tired of this adventure now.

"Hey, come on, Ron! If you quit now, then I'll be the only guy here," Josh protested.

"You have Pete," Ron grumbled.

"But you're on your own. I'm staying put. I want this adventure too, even if it means I'll be scared," Pal said defiantly.

"Noo-o!" Ron moaned. "Urgghh! You guys are always one-sided! Can't anyone be on my side for once?" he whined.

"No," Carra said, rolling her eyes.

"I've been standing up for you for as long as I can remember," Pal added sweetly.

"Except you,"

"No," Carra repeated.

"Urgghhh!" Ron felt like screaming so loudly that Grinlaut himself would run away.

"Come on. We've a mission to complete," May ordered.

"Is it not 'mission to accomplish'?" Ron heard Ivy asking May as he trudged along, feeling like falling on the path.

"Hey, you don't have to do anything, you know. Nothing at all. Just help us out a little, then you can run away, you know," Iris whispered to Ron as she jogged past to catch up with her sister, who was sprinting into the cave already.

"Really?" He asked, brightening up at once.

"Shut up!" Tabitha and Victoria hissed at him.

"Sorry,"

"Come on in fast, slowpoke," Tabitha growled at him.

"I'm *not* a slowpoke!" Ron protested.

"Keep quiet!" Victoria snarled.

Ron did manage to stay quiet throughout the whole process of entering the rock. They immediately set their plan in action. Josh scuttled over to an entrance which was big enough to host all their hostages and peeked in, but instantly hurried out. "Grinlaut's in there! Thank God, he was asleep. No one saw me,"

"Then the prisoners should be down, in the cellar," Iris breathed. "You are right, Sister. Go check it!" Ivy sent Josh and Carra to check the cellar. May and Iris were to stand guard, with Ruben and Snowflake. Pete and Tabitha went with Josh and Carra. Ivy, Victoria, Pal and Ron stayed hidden as back-up. All the guards were most probably in the one-hundred-and-one rooms in the rock.

"Stay quiet!" Ivy hissed, but Ron could not stop chattering his teeth and shivering in fear.

Suddenly, Iris sprang forward and grabbed Carra. "I forgot to tell you. Beware, for Grinlaut's wife may be lurking down there," she warned. "Jesus! Now he has a wife, too?" Josh said, sounding exasperated. "God, next he'll have a bomb son and a killer daughter!"

"He does have a son and a daughter, but they are quite friendly and detest their father. They might prove as a formidable ally," Iris confirmed.

"Jesus Christ!" Josh smacked his head with his head. "This wife of his, what about her?" Carra asked cautiously.

"If she is in a cage, she is a friend. If she is in the water, she is a foe," Iris explained, then gave them a firm push. "Go, now!"

Grinlaut's wife was not what they were expecting. Not at all. They knew they couldn't hope to find his wife something like a human after what Iris said about her being in water, but they couldn't even imagine that his wife would be a *crocodile,* with hoofs and a turtle shell. She *was* locked up in a cage, and she was crying a moat. They realised she was his wife, for she had a mark, which most probably came from a heated rod, saying 'Agrid, His Most Excellency's Wife' on her arm. They did not disturb her, and moved on to the next cage. There, a handsome boy and a beautiful girl were sitting on the floor and talking. The boy looked very normal, except for his unusual pointed, dark blue finger nails, and for his thick, brown hair which looked like it shimmered with electricity. He even had weird, paw-like feet. The girl, however, seemed to have light green wings, and cat-like ears and eyes. She had light blonde hair, which had somehow merged up with her arm's hair, and so, moved in whichever direction she moved her hand. The other cells were empty. No Ronens had been locked up there.

"Has she put some sort of adhesive or glue to her hair? I wonder which brand she used," Though Josh whispered this;

the girl turned back sharply and showed her pointed teeth. The boy too, hissed as his teeth enlarged, becoming like a sabre-toothed tigers' teeth. His hair spiked up instantly, and his whole head buzzed with lightning, illuminating his hair every now and then, making it a very light blonde for a few seconds.

"Hel-" Carra started to scream, but Josh quickly shut her mouth. They saw that, these kids too, had a mark. The boy had 'Lykenzer, His Most Excellency's Son', and the girl had 'Zevyn, His Most Excellency's Daughter'. For the first time, Josh realized that it was written in English. Carra had the same thought at exactly the same moment. But that was not the time to think about languages, they had to save their skin first.

Josh immediately shouted, "Stop, Lykenzsar and Zevny or whatever your names are! We have come to help you! We have come from Earth!" He shouted, then said more quietly, "Hope you know what that is,"

"How did you know? You came close to our names. Did He tell you to come and take us up? Did he? Speak, Earthling!" The boy shouted. His hair still hummed with electricity, but his teeth had shrunk back to their normal size. The girl furled her wings behind her back and stopped hissing, too. She raised her ears with curiosity.

"No, no! You've got it all wrong! Grinlaut didn't send us, we came to rescue his kids and wife and his prisoners, the Ronens. Yes, the Ronens!" Carra repeated, to highlight the tall task they had ahead.

"Are you alone-" the boy started again, but the girl had crept up and interrupted him. "What are your names?" She asked shyly.

"Zevyn, be quiet. We need to learn more about them. We cannot trust them yet!" he hissed.

"That is exactly why we need to know their names!" She growled back.

But they were both cut off by an alarming shriek. "Josh, Carra! Get out of there now! Right NOW!"

"May!" Carra whispered. "Come on!" Tabitha urged. Only then was that the boy and Zevyn noticed the cat and bird.

"Wait! Free us!" He cried suddenly, as if the bird and cat were of such importance.

"Is someone giving you a feast down there? Get out!" Ruben screamed. The ceiling and the floor rumbled as he shouted the warning. Josh lost his balance, and fell down, banging his hand to the cage bars. It swelled up, but he didn't bother. He just picked himself up, dusted himself and inspected his arm. It wasn't serious; he would ask the doctor what to do later. But Zevyn just touched his arm and it became normal again! He looked at her, puzzled, but she just shook her head.

Pete flew straight to the cage door and picked it with his claws.

"What's keeping you boneheads? You need more warnings?" Pal cried.

"We can't get out! The ceiling- it's caving in! What do we do?" Carra yelled back.

"Get out somehow!" Ivy called. "It is an earthquake!"

"Shouldn't that be 'Imagneusquake'?" Josh asked.

"Can someone slap him for me?" May called.

"Please, come out quickly!" Snowflake's pleading voice echoed around, even though she uttered it softly. Suddenly the sound of running feet was heard, and an agonizing howl. "Ron, come back!" Iris yelled, and the sound of her and Pal running echoed throughout the dungeon- cellar.

"I can help you!" Zevyn said. "Hold my hands," She instructed Carra. "The parrot can take him," She said, nodding to Josh. "Lykenzer, use your lightning and get the cat out," She said and gripped Carra's hands as she unfurled her wings and started flapping.

"What about the crocodile?" Carra asked as they flew up, over the stairs.

"You mean Mother? Lyke will take care of her. Don't worry. Mother's not as delicate as she might seem," Zevyn assured her.

By the time they reached the ground level, Carra's arms felt like they would come out of their sockets. "Oww," She groaned. Not soon after, Pete came up, dragging Josh by his hands with obvious effort. Pete seemed to be a bit bigger. In fact, he was bigger, almost Pal's size. Ruben immediately came to Pete's aid and seized Josh's shoulders. The parrot let go, relieved, as Ruben dragged the boy to safety.

"Come on, we have to go! Where is Tab-" Ivy started, but then she noticed Zevyn, and stopped. "Who are you?" she hissed. "No time! Lyke will be here with the cat. We have to get out! Father will not spare you!" Zevyn urged, pushing Iris and Carra.

"Wait. You are Grinlaut's daughter?" Iris asked in amazement.

"Yes! And he will have your skins if you don't get out! My brother will be here with the cat! Now go! Please," She pleaded. "Best get out," May agreed, and dashed out, with Snowflake at her heels. Josh beat her to the door though, and Pete was out a second later. But May didn't make it out; she slipped and fell, and Snowflake tried to help her get up. Nothing had happened to her though, and she jogged a bit painfully in the direction of the door. Iris had left Pal and Ron out, and there they were, astounded to see a strange girl with green wings, their mouths open and eyes bulging.

"Get out of here!" Pete literally screeched right into Ron and Pal's ears.

"Yeeooww!" Ron screamed as he scrambled to get his footing.

"Why?" Pal called back as he dashed to the safety of the bushes. "Because the world is falling apart!" Pete cried, flapping his wigs in a deranged manner.

"Shut up, Pete! You are driving me insane!" Ivy screamed from inside the stone. May had not yet made it outside, and Carra was helping her friend. It was total chaos inside the rock. Strangely, the guards and Grinlaut still did not seem to know what was going on. 'They must be heavy sleepers.' Carra thought. 'Either that, or they would be in the weaponry, getting ready for battle.' Suddenly, thunder boomed and a lightning bolt crackled outside the sky. It struck the giant rock and smashed it into smithereens. Everybody screamed, as they crouched down and hid their heads in their hands. But magically, not one piece fell on any of them. Iris looked up and saw Zevyn in a blurry of wings. She was flapping her wings so fast that it repelled every little tiny rock and sent it flying into the sides. Slowly, one by one, the rest looked up too, as Zevyn worked wonders. Her brother showed up too, encased in a ball of lightning which protected himself, Tabitha whom he carried, and the crocodile who was standing by his side.

"Lyke! Help me!" Zevyn cried. "I'm coming Zevyn! Hold on!" He left the shield, but it stayed enclosed around Tabitha and the crocodile, who, apparently, was his mother.

He raced across to the middle of the room, faster than lightning, and sent an electrical bolt to the sky, gripping the ground tightly with his back leg paws. That bolt reached the point where the former ceiling was, then divided itself into many parts, which flew in every direction, consuming the left out rocks and stones. When it reached the ground, it was merely a tiny spark which dissolved into thin air. His sister stopped flapping and descended slowly, looking very dizzy.

"Thanks, Lyke," She whispered. When she reached the ground, she crumpled, barely even moving, save for the continuous rise and fall of her stomach, showing that she was alive. Lykenzer and the crocodile immediately raced to her side. Bits of rock still jutted out, and the floor of the rock was almost gone, the cellar in clear sight.

"What happened?" Tabitha asked cautiously.

"You, parrot. Get some water," Lykenzer ordered Pete, who had just flown inside.

As Pete flew away, the creature next to Lyke become more human like and less like a crocodile. Her shell started shrinking until it disappeared, and her snout also shrivelled until a distinct green human-like nose could be seen. Next, her colour started changing. It became more of peach and beige colours mixed. Her hoofs faded away as she stood upright, changing into hands and feet. She turned into a fair lady, pretty tall, maybe about 5.5 feet. She had piercing orange eyes, which seemed to blaze with fire which was alive.

"Zevyn?" she asked. She shook the girl's shoulder gently. Her voice was as melodious as a nightingale's. She kneeled down, stroking Zevyn's cheek. "Mother?" Zevyn said drowsily. She opened one sleepy eye, which soon widened with surprise. She struggled to sit up as she tried to open the other eye. It had, seemingly, got stuck together; a tiny effect of being struck by Lykenzer's lightning and because all her energy was drained out. She finally managed it, and sat on her knees with a look of bewilderment on her face. Pete came back at that moment, and dropped the bucket of water in surprise. Victoria jumped nimbly into the air to catch him as he floated down, losing control over his wings on seeing Lyke's and Zevyn's mother.

"Stop, everyone! Nobody will move, unless you want to get burned," A rough, coarse voice commanded.

"Now who's that?" Ron grumbled as he walked in sleepily. But the lazy look was wiped right off his face at the sight he saw. There was Grinlaut, with his soldiers pointing something like a big tube connected to a fireball at one end at him. There was a strange lady, bending over the winged girl. And another boy, with animal- like hazel eyes sitting next to them.

"Whoa! Sorry! Don't blow me up!" Ron screamed at Grinlaut and the soldier.

"Shut up, human!" Grinlaut roared, his stinky breath reaching May and Ruben, who gagged.

"Technically, I'm a Ronen now," Ron pouted.

"No you're not. Minkin said we need to do that ritual again," Josh pointed out.

"Enough nonsense!"Grinlaut snarled. "Judkinn, both be killed!"

A guard flexed his muscles, which seemed to be about 3 inches big, and took aim. He was just about to shoot when a cry distracted him.

"You cannot kill him that easily," A vaguely familiar voice said.

"Father!"Ivy and Iris cried at once.

"Attack!" Avaron cried, charging through a window-like structure which had formed after the rock crumpled, with a sword in hand. Chester raced alongside him. Leif and Romial came next, but Leif changed direction and ran towards his sisters.

"Leif!" Iris cried, running forward to hug him. Ivy followed.

"Don't forget Iris, I have to push you once," He said, smiling. "What?" Iris asked, confused. "You pushed me when we first came here, didn't you?" He asked, hugging his sister.

"Later, later," Iris turned around. "Zevyn? Are you all right?" she asked, giving the girl a hand to get up.

"Yeah, sort of. You, Lyke? Mother?" she turned to her own family. For a time, they forgot that a battle was being waged around them. They were all lost until Avaron finally called out to his son "Leif! What in the Ronen's name are you doing? Come and help us here!" He shouted.

"Carra! Ron!" Another voice reached them, a desperate shout. The cousins whipped their heads around just in time to see Carra's father being wrestled by a soldier.

"Dad!" Carra yelled. She ran and jumped on the guard's back, aided by Tabitha and her father's bond.The kingfisher, Carra's father's bond, flew straight over and pecked the guard's head.

"Ow!" the guard cried, dropping his weapon to hold his head. Pal immediately raced over and seized the fire gun, only to be knocked out from his mouth by a Hikint who accidently kicked him while fighting. It flew straight into the air. Ruben and Pete dove for it at the same time and crashed into each other instead of catching the gun. Victoria leaped up and caught the gun firmly between her teeth, but before she could touch the ground, a strong guard hurled across the room and caught her, making her drop the gun. It flew straight towards Ivy, but she didn't notice because she was running to help her bond. But what it did fall on was Crocphant's head, and he was knocked out a third time. May sprinted to it, but a deer beat her to it, knocking a soldier out of its way with it humongous antlers.

He passed it over to his bond, who aimed it at the nearest soldier. "Yu donat eva no how to yoose it," The dog faced pig soldier snickered.

"You don't even know how to speak," The Ronen smirked, and smacked the gun's fire end on the soldier's stomach. The dog-pig howled in pain, and went limp. The Ronen smiled in satisfaction and flung the gun in the same way at another soldier, watching him burn as he collapsed in a heap.

At that moment, Ivy came running to him. "Where's

Father?" she panted out of breath.

"He is there," he said, pointing. "Thanks," She said, and dashed off again.

"Father!" she called, but a flurry of wings stopped her from continuing. "Zevyn! Let me go!" Ivy whispered, for she was out of breath.

"Look where you run, and then tell me to not save your life," Zevyn hissed. Ivy looked up and saw two guards. They were being hurled around, thrown inside a tornado, which Zevyn had created with the wind from her wings.

"Thank you, Zevyn, but my sister is dying," Ivy rasped.

"Who? Iris?" Zevyn asked, letting go at once.

"No, my youngest sister, Lily," Ivy answered, standing up. She raced off with the other girl by her side to find Avaron.

"Father!" Ivy cried as they finally found him.

"What happened?" Avaron asked. "Is it Lily?"

Ivy nodded between tears. "Minkin!" Avaron called at once, and the three (Zevyn went back to fighting) rushed to where Iris and Leif were kneeling next to the unconscious body of their sister. "Lily," Avaron whispered. Minkin immediately set to work. He quickly removed the arrow which had struck the girl while muttering some chant. He was still whispering the spell to himself when he held the arrow, and when he finished, it vanished! So did the wound on Lily's stomach!

"Daddy?" she struggled to sit up. "Daddy!" she squealed, looking more frightened than pleased to see her father. "Father! Behind you!" Iris shrieked this time. Avaron immediately turned, and saw a creepy grin turn to confusion as Misty, Lily's bat rescued Avaron from a donkey-faced spider. His spear was yanked out of his pincer hand as Misty screeched and clawed him until he fell unconscious from the number of scratches present on his body. And as they watched, more and more Hikints, or the soldiers were falling, and twice that number of Ronens rising. They were winning!

But so what if they were more in number? If Grinlaut was dealt with only would this battle meet an end. Avaron helped and thanked Misty and walked calmly to Grinlaut, who was trying to escape unseen. Realising that he was being followed, he turned to a sprint, which came to an abrupt halt as a lion came and blocked him. Chester was all in all terrifying, every bit of him, from his newly sharpened teeth and claws, to his menacing, gigantic mane, to his bristling fur, to his razor spiked tail.

"Chester, where did you get those spikes?" Avaron asked, amused and a bit surprised.

"Oh, that. I just stole a few from Grinlaut's back when he wasn't looking," Chester said, inspecting his paw casually, showing all his blade-like claws. Grinlaut squeaked and looked down his back. Sure enough, half of his spikes were missing.

"Looking good, Grinlaut," Romial grinned, striding over. Grinlaut looked terrified. But it was soon overcome by anger. 'How dare they do this?' he thought. "How!?" he screeched, and lunged towards Romial, who was caught off guard. Too bad for Grinlaut, though, because the Ronen who had killed the Hikints with the fire-gun mentioned earlier, came to the scene and threw the fire gun at Grinlaut, which hit the monster square on his cheek horn, cutting it into half. He yelped in pain, but that was enough distraction for the Ronen leaders. Avaron took a big spear he found nearby, and whacked Grinlaut heavily on the back with the wooden side of the spear. Grinlaut was sent flying and Chester caught him full on, and the other cheek horn and one of his head horns broke. Grinlaut fell with a thump, and before anyone could anything else, a woman hurried over, dressed in white, and they guessed she was the beast's wife. She grabbed the spear from a surprised Avaron's hands and stabbed Grinlaut, ending his miserable life.

"Finally," She sighed, looking at a mark on her arm. The seal that marked her as Grinlaut's wife faded away, not even leaving a mark. The same happened to Lyke and Zevyn. Zevyn's hair became detached from her arms, and Lyke's long lost brown wolf-tail grew back. The standing Hikints remaining looked around in astonishment as their minds cleared. They had been hypnotised by their former evil master, and now they all walked towards him, each kicking or stabbing the lifeless body.

As the Hikints started to return to their own homeland, a bright flash blinded everyone, a flash so bright that all of them were seeing spots even after a minute the flash disappeared. As they watched, Ronens started appearing in the entrance of the clearing, led by a woman wearing a white dress. She had long, black, curly hair, and the olive green eyes that marked her as a Ronen. She was thin, but looked quite strong, strong enough to defeat a lion with her bare hands.

"Who's that?" Carra asked May, but they both knew the answer. And they were even more sure when Iris and Ivy raced forward, shouting "Mother! You came back! Mother!"

